For Adam Enjoy the book!
Happy Holidays. John

A VINCE TORELLI NOVEL BOOK 2: RETRIBUTION

By John Schembra

John R. Schembra

Writers Exchange E-Publishing
http://www.writers-exchange.com/

A Vince Torelli Novel Book 2: Retribution

Writers Exchange E-Publishing
PO Box 372
ATHERTON QLD 4883

Cover Art: Laura Shinn

Published by Writers Exchange E-Publishing
http://www.writers-exchange.com

ISBN Print: 1876962682 (WEE)

Retribution ***n.*** To repay; punishment for evil done; requital

Chapter 1

He looked at his watch, noting it was 10:34 pm. He rolled the naked body out the back of the van, closed the rear doors, and drove slowly through the alley, stopping at the crosswalk before turning onto 5th Street. Looking to his left, he saw the two beat officers walking toward him at a leisurely pace. He smiled to himself as he thought of what awaited them if they took their usual route down the alley. He turned right on 5th Street, then right again on Folsom, driving at the speed limit, attracting no unwanted attention from the few other motorists.

He had no fear of being identified. He was just an ordinary looking guy driving an ordinary looking van. He had left no clues in the alley that could lead to him and no one had seen him. Besides, he had stopped perhaps thirty seconds, just long enough to dump the body, and the van he was driving would not be reported stolen from the Oakland airport long term parking lot for a couple of days.

He had spent the last several evenings watching the two cops walking their Mission District beat. He had mapped and timed their route, finding they were creatures of habit, stopping for dinner at the same time each night, always at one of the small restaurants along Mission Street. After resuming their foot patrol, they entered the alley between 10:30 and

10:36 p.m. each night. He saw there was little vehicle traffic during the week and few people on the street. He also knew there were no homeless people living in the alley and it was not a place the drug dealers chose to ply their trade. It was the perfect place to put the body so it could be "found" quickly, exactly as he planned.

He drove to Pacific Heights and parked the van along the curb between two of the stately homes. He walked the half block to his Lexus, taking off the latex gloves as he walked and dropping them in a sewer near his parked car. He glanced up and down the street as he unlocked the door, seeing no one and no lights on in the nearby homes. He started the car and drove leisurely out of the area, unable to stop smiling. He felt good, strong, revitalized. He was filled with a sense of accomplishment, of relief that justice had been served. He could hardly wait to start planning the next event. He turned the radio up and drove slowly home through the damp San Francisco night, singing to the oldies.

Chapter 2

The incessant ringing of the phone next to his bed dragged him from his slumber. Without opening his eyes, he groped for the phone. Bringing the receiver up to his ear, he mumbled, "This better be good."

"C'mon, Vince. Would I be calling the eminent homicide inspector Torelli at this hour if it wasn't? You're gonna love this."

"Shit," he said, opening his eyes and looking at the clock as he recognized the night watch homicide inspector's voice. He reached over and turned on the light next to the bed. "Geez, Jimmy, it's 12:45 in the morning. What's so important that you just had to call me?"

"You awake Vince? You listening to me?"

"Yeah, Yeah, Jimmy. So what's the news?"

"A couple of beat cops found a body in an alley off 5th Street. A young male, Hispanic, all sliced up."

"So what's all this got to do with me?"

"Easy, big fella. The victim just happens to be a very bad boy himself. Not the kinda guy too many people are gonna miss. In fact, he just dodged a murder charge when the witness against him disappeared."

"Jimmy, it's too early in the morning for guessing games. Just tell me who, OK?"

"Alright, alright! You remember that little rat-faced punk, Julio Barajas? Did that drive-by on Wallace Street a few months ago in which he missed his target and killed that three-year-old boy walking with his mother? Well, somebody did him tonight, and from the looks of him, whoever it was must have been mighty pissed off."

"Really? Julio Barajas, eh? Well, can't say I'm sorry he got whacked. If anybody deserved it, he did."

"Yeah, for sure. I guess somebody had a major grudge against him. You know, it really pissed me off he beat that kid's murder. The only witness takes off and he walks. I guess there is a God after all, eh Vince?"

"Yep. Divine intervention, Jimmy. You need any help? Want me to come in?"

"Nah. Go back to sleep. I'll see ya in the morning and fill you in on the details then. Not much else to do tonight. No witnesses, no obvious evidence, so get some rest. See ya in a few hours."

Vince hung up the phone and turned off the light.

"Do you have to go in?" his wife asked.

"No. Jimmy just called to fill me in on a homicide I'll be getting in the morning. Remember that case Mike and I worked last year, the drive by at Hunters Point where the three year old boy was killed?"

"Yes. You got the shooter, didn't you, when the passenger came forward?"

"That's the one. The guy beat the rap because the witness disappeared. He walked last month. He was the victim. Mike is gonna dance a jig when he hears. He really took this case personally. Remember how pissed he was when the D.A. refused to file charges?"

"Yes. I remember very well. He came over here and was ranting and raving for a half hour! Well, what goes around comes around, honey."

"Yeah. Now I gotta try to solve this one. Pretty ironic, isn't it. First I try to prosecute the guy, now I gotta find out who killed him."

"You better get some sleep, then. Something tells me this one isn't going to be easy."

"Yeah. G'nite, babe."

"'Nite, honey." She leaned in and kissed him on the cheek, snuggled down under the blankets and in less than a minute her breathing had become deep and regular.

Vince lay in bed listening to her breathe, thinking about what faced him in the morning. He had difficulty getting back to sleep, as he often did when awakened in the middle of the night. His thoughts turned to his past, his time in Vietnam and how he came to join the police department, and sleep would evade him sometimes for hours.

He remembered the attack on the airbase, hearing the explosions and feeling the shock and pain of his wounds, seeing the bodies of the enemy he killed.

With the encouragement of his father, he applied to the San Francisco Police Department. He was scheduled to start the police academy in April.

Vince found the academy training easy enough. He liked the camaraderie that developed between the recruits, and was happier than he had been for some time. It reminded him of his time in the army and he became focused again, dwelling less and less on his time in Nam. The dreams became less frequent, and he was often able to sleep through the night.

Chapter 3

The morning started like any other. The boys were at breakfast, arguing over who was the best all-time baseball player, Hank Aaron or Willie Mays. It was already 72 degrees out, promising to be a hot day. Maggie was spooning scrambled eggs on a plate while Vince poured himself a cup of coffee. He ate quickly, knowing he had a long day ahead of him.

"Dad, who do you think the greatest ball player was?" his youngest son Scott asked. "Willie Mays or Hank Aaron?"

"Michael Jordan."

"Aw, c'mon, Dad," both boys said in unison.

"I still think it's Michael Jordan, and I'm not gonna get caught in the middle of your argument."

His wife leaned over and whispered in his ear. "Coward."

"Yep," he said, grabbing her and planting a kiss on her cheek. "I gotta get going. Got a mess waiting for me."

"Will you be home for dinner?" Maggie asked.

"I wouldn't count on it. I've got a feeling this is just the start of something big. I"ll call you later and let you know."

"Okay, Babe. You be careful."

***

Vince was at his desk, drinking his second cup of coffee, reading the preliminary reports when his boss, Lieutenant Simons, walked up. "Anything jump out at you?" he asked, sitting on the corner of the desk.

"Not really. Hardly any evidence and no witnesses. The one question I have is why was he dumped there? He obviously was killed somewhere else, so why did the killer pick that spot to dump the body? Barajas doesn't live in that area, and to our knowledge, never comes down to the Mission district."

"Opportunity?"

"I don't think so, Boss. There are an awful lot of better places to dump a body in this city. It's almost as if the killer wanted it to be found."

"Well, if that's true, why?"

"I don't know yet. If I had to guess, I'd say he was telling us how easy this murder was, and that there may be more to come."

"So, what's the plan?"

"I've got Wilson on the computer running all of Barajas' known associates, plus any previous arrests. Maybe he has an enemy in a rival gang, or he pissed off one of his own gangbangers. I'd go talk to the family of the little boy Barajas killed except they moved to Fresno. I've got one of the Fresno detectives going out to the house to see if they are all there, none of 'em missing or on a trip, and to interview them, but I don't think this has to do with the family."

"Why? You know something we don't?"

"No, just a hunch. Something doesn't figure with this. I keep asking myself why he was dumped where he was. As I said, it's almost as if the killer wanted him to be found. And if that's true, why?"

"I'm assigning Clark full time to help you with this. Let's see if we can close this one out quickly. Shouldn't be too hard. A guy like Barajas has a lot of enemies, so it's just a matter of finding the right one."

"I wish it were that simple. Well, time to hit the bricks. I'll keep you posted."

Vince and Clark spent the rest of the morning finding and interviewing Barajas' known associates. No one had any idea who would want to kill him, other than a rival gang member, and Vince was convinced this was not a gang killing. He had worked with Clark on over two dozen cases since Clark had joined the homicide division five years earlier. The first homicide he worked was with Vince, who took him under his wing and taught him the ropes. Clark admired and respected Vince, and learned much from him. He took every opportunity to work with him, and they soon became close friends, spending most of their on-duty time and some of their off-duty time together.

They had become such close friends that one day at lunch, Vince opened up and told Clark about his time in Vietnam, something he had never done with anyone but Maggie. In turn, Clark told Vince that he had joined the Mendocino Sheriff's Department two years after his brother was stabbed to death while trying to break up a fight at the Buckhorn Bar in Willits, where he worked. The murderer was never caught, and as soon as he was old enough, Clark applied for the deputy job. After four years, he applied to and was accepted at the San Francisco Police Department, eventually working his way up to the homicide division.

After lunch they went to the morgue for the autopsy. The Medical Examiner, Doctor Chamberlin, had been performing autopsies for 18 years and had seen things most people could not even imagine. He was munching on an apple and writing at a small desk as Vince and Clark walked in the room. Barajas' body lay on a gurney being cleaned up by an assistant prior to being taken back to the morgue.

"Hey, Doc," Vince said as he entered. "Still selling body parts on the side?"

Doctor Chamberlin looked up from his notepad. "You wait, Torelli. You'll see how expensive it is to have two kids in college. Gotta make ends meet somehow."

"How's our friend Barajas?"

"Dead, and I mean *really* dead. Somebody had some fun with this one. Whoever did this was very upset with this young man. Bled him out pretty good before killing him."

"Oh, yeah? How so?"

"For starters, he made 37 cuts all over the body, some pretty deep, all would have been very painful and bled a lot, but weren't fatal. Probably would have been, had the cuts been made all at once, but it appears they were made over some period of time.

There's coagulation in different stages in some of them which would indicate others were fresher, probably made after the first cuts stopped bleeding."

"Any estimate, Doc, on how long it would have taken the killer?" Vince asked, sitting down on a chair next to the desk.

"Hard to say. I would estimate at least a couple of hours. He was tied and gagged." He looked at Vince and Mike, grinning at their looks of puzzlement. "How does he know this, you ask? I found ligature bruising on his wrists and ankles, and residue from tape on his mouth. Duct tape, I'd say, if you asked my opinion."

"Brilliant, Doc. Then he was tortured before being killed?"

"I'd say so. Then, after the killer tired of his little game, he administered the coup de gras by stabbing him with a very sharp knife in the heart. The blade entered just below the xyphoid process in an upward and slightly left direction into the heart. The killer then moved the knife back and forth, lacerating the heart muscle, hence causing the ultimate demise of poor Mr. Barajas."

"Would Barajas still have been conscious at that point?"

"Probably, though very weak from loss of blood. I understand there was not much blood around the body, and since there wasn't much left *in* the body, I deduce he was killed somewhere else. I am right, am I not, Watson?"

"Good work, Sherlock. What would we poor, dull witted investigators do without the benefit of your wisdom, Doc? Clark, can't you just feel the wisdom in this room?" Vince grinned at his partner, who just nodded in agreement. "How long ago did he die?"

"He was found around 10:30 pm, so I'd say he died at least two or three hours earlier."

"That would make it between 7:30 and 8:30 p.m. last night. We know the alley was clear around nine when the beat cops walked through it, so the question is, where did the killer keep the body all that time, and where was he killed?"

Clark, who had been listening, chimed in. "Do you think the killer could have been driving around with the body all that time?"

"No, I don't think so," Vince replied. "Too much chance of something going wrong. What if a traffic cop stopped him? Or maybe got in an accident? No, I think Barajas was killed not too far away from where he was dumped. C'mon, Clark, let's go check it out. Thanks, Doc. As always, your sage advice has opened a few doors."

"As always, you are welcome. Oh, one last thing. There was a shallow cut on his cheek that didn't fit the other cuts."

"How so?"

"Well, it was superficial and didn't fit the pattern of the other cuts. All the others were made to inflict pain and blood loss. This cut looks suspiciously like the number one."

"Does it just look like it, or is it actually the number?"

"Hard to tell. Skin is elastic, so it's a bit distorted, but it does appear to be a number. Don't quote me on that, but it very well could be a sign."

"I'll keep it in mind. One last thing, Doc. What can you tell me about the knife?"

"Only that it was large and very sharp. From the fatal stab wound, I'd say it was like a hunting knife, maybe a Bowie knife. The blade had to be at least six inches long and a bit more than an inch wide, maybe an inch and a quarter. A formidable weapon, Vince, designed to intimidate and terrorize as well as kill."

"If we find the weapon, would you be able to match it to the wounds?" Clark asked.

"Maybe, Mike. Probably couldn't make a positive match, but I may be able to say the wounds are consistent with the weapon."

"Guess that will have to do," Vince said. "Thanks, Doc. We've got to go. Call me if you find anything else of interest."

As Vince turned to leave, Dr. Chamberlin put his hand on his shoulder. "Hey, Vince, be careful with this one, okay? Whoever did this is pretty disturbed and extremely dangerous."

"We will, Doc. Thanks again."

As they left, Vince called his office and had three uniform officers assigned to him for the rest of the afternoon. He had them meet him where the body had been found. When his mini-taskforce had been formed, he gathered them around.

"Here's what I need. You will be doing a canvass of the area looking for the possible murder site from the homicide last night. Don't worry about any buildings that are open to the public or business offices that are used every day. We are looking for empty or abandoned buildings, basements, construction sites, whatever. You will know you have the right place when you find a large amount of blood, some sort of ropes, wires, or ties, and tape. Everyone go to channel 4 on your portables and report directly to me if you find something. If you do find a possible crime scene, don't touch or move anything, just secure the area and notify me. Clark, you start your canvass one block south. You, Officer...?" Vince asked, pointing at one of the uniforms.

"Coleman, Inspector."

"Coleman, start one block west."

Turning to the other two officers, he said, "And you are?"

"Officers Mattox and Berenson, Inspector."

"Officer Mattox, you start one block north, and Berenson, one block east." Turning back to the group, he said, "If you don't find anything, then widen the search another block, then another. In any case, limit your search to a five-block radius. When you complete the search, start interviewing anyone who appears to be local to the area. In particular, people who may be out and about at odd hours, street people, homeless, druggies, whatever. Find out if anyone saw anything, anyone, or any vehicles that did not belong in their neighborhood. Make sure you ID them properly and know how to get a hold of them later if you need to. It is now 2:30. We will meet back here at seven p.m. Any questions? No? Then let's go."

Chapter 4

Shooting Suspect Ruled Mentally Incompetent
By Liz Maltby, Staff Writer

The San Francisco District Attorney's Office announced today that no criminal charges would be filed against the 16-year-old suspect in the shooting at Masterson High School that killed a teacher and three students and left five other students wounded, two critically. Two psychiatric evaluations determined the suspect, whose name is not being released due to his age, is so mentally disturbed he was unable to tell right from wrong at the time of the shooting.

Prosecutors argued that the suspect knew exactly what he was doing and planned the assault days ahead of time, even confiding to a friend what he planned to do. The alleged motive was revenge against the teacher and two of the dead students for excluding him from an art project he wanted to be involved with. "The fact that this young man stole the gun three days before the shooting, hiding it in an unused locker at school along with over 100 rounds of ammunition, had made threats to the victims at least two days prior to the killings, and had dropped hints to friends of his intentions shows a purposeful pre-plan by a methodical, clear thinking mind."

In spite of those arguments, the 16-year-old student was remanded to the psychiatric ward at San Francisco General Hospital for further evaluation. He is scheduled to be trans-

ferred from the juvenile hall to Atascadero State Hospital within the next week.

He read the article three times, seething with anger. Slamming the paper down on the van's seat, he muttered, "I can't fucking believe this. With all the evidence showing he knew what he was doing, he's not gonna go to trial. God damn liberal judges and god damn defense attorneys. He's got to be held accountable, and if it can't be through the criminal justice system, then it will be through other means! And not releasing his name? Shit, everyone knows his name. Murderous little bastard. He will have to pay for what he has done!" He drove home quickly, anxious to begin planning the demise of one Mitch Ballinger, sixteen-year-old multiple murderer.

Knowing the hospital was classified as a maximum security facility and that visitors would have to show identification, sign in, pass through a metal detector and be subjected to a thorough search presented him with a unique situation. He paced the floor of his spacious living room, mulling over the potential problems he was facing in getting his hands on Mitch Ballinger. He knew once the subject arrived at Atascadero he would be virtually untouchable. That left him with only two options. Take him before he was transferred, or take him somewhere along the road. He decided to take him along the way to minimize the risk to himself. To go after him while he was still at the hospital in San Francisco would mean he would have to use a disguise and present a false ID. That would get him in, but how would he get the both of them out? He did not want to kill him in the hospital. He wanted some time alone with him to make him realize the error of his ways, as he had with the pig Barajas. He wanted to bleed him, make him suffer, then give him hope before crushing that hope and striking the final blow to snuff out his worthless, miserable life. He smiled at that, remembering how Barajas had cried with relief when he thought he would be let go, and the look of shock on his face when the knife was driven into his heart.

He knew the procedure for transferring a mental patient to Atascadero State Hospital and he was certain there would only be one guard and a technician from the hospital, plus the driver, instead of two armed guards usually assigned for the most dangerous prisoners. After all, this was a sixteen-year-old boy. He would have to scout the route down Hwy 101, finding the best place to set the ambush. He would need some special equipment to disable the van and neutralize the guards, something that would act quickly. He did not want to harm the guard or technician unless it was absolutely necessary. He only wanted to take Mitch with him when he left, take him to the room where he could be alone with him for a few hours. He already knew where he would dump the body, and he smiled to himself, thinking how ironic it would be when they found him. He was anticipating the feeling of accomplishment and closure he would experience when he was done with this one. He picked up the phone and dialed a number, humming softly while it rang.

Chapter 5

Vince Torelli sat in the homicide division conference room, briefing his boss, Lieutenant Simons, on the Barajas investigation.

"I'll tell you, Boss, I'm stumped by this one. Usually by now we have enough information to figure out why he was killed, but no one seems to know anything about this. Even my contacts in the gangs haven't heard anything, not even rumors of who could have killed Barajas."

"Are these contacts reliable?"

"Yeah. I'm sure this was not gang related or they would have passed the info on to me. And I'm certain the little boy's family was not involved. They're still in Fresno and the cops there have been able to verify no one from the family was out of the area at the time of the murder. There are no other relatives in the Bay Area, and we interviewed all the parents' neighbors. Turns out they didn't have any close friends here, kept mainly to themselves. They had only lived in the neighborhood about four months before the little boy was killed."

"Any luck in finding the murder scene?"

"No. We canvassed several blocks around the dump site, and talked with most of the locals in the area with no luck."

"Any evidence found at the scene or on the body?"

"Nothing of any value. Some dirt and mud on his feet. We've sent that to the lab to see what it contains. It might give us an idea of where to look, but other than that, nothing. We had the body fingerprinted, found a partial on the guy's shoulder."

"Really? Good. Can we identify it?"

"Not much to work with, but, yes, I think so. The print guys said there was enough detail to identify the person who left it there if we ever find him."

"Let's get the fingerprint guys to check all their databases, including the FBI, county, and some of the larger police departments in the Bay Area. Let me know if you find anything."

"Sure will, Boss. I've gotta check out a few things, so I'm gonna get going."

"All right. Keep me informed, Torelli."

Though Lieutanant Simons appeared gruff and impatient, Vince, and the other inspectors in the homicide division, knew he was fair and would always back them in how they conducted their investigations. Lieutenant Simons did not want to appear soft or too friendly, as he felt the inspectors may tend to take advantage of his good nature, so he adopted the gruff manner as a proactive measure. He didn't fool anyone.

Vince rose, then paused at the door. "One thing I do know. I think there's more to this than just a simple murder of a gangbanger. Doc Chamberlin found a cut on Barajas' cheek he thinks is the number one. He can't be sure, and I hope he's wrong, 'cause if he isn't, this is just the first murder by this psycho. We don't need another serial killer on our hands, and whoever did this was too careful, took extra time to make sure there would be no useful evidence. The murder was committed someplace he or she didn't want us to find, and dumping the body in a different location effectively eliminated most of the evidence. Whoever did this might have some knowledge of evidence procedures and forensics."

"That could be anyone from a cop to a criminal justice student, to someone who reads a lot. You can get that info off the internet, for Gods' sake. That thinking could be a dead end."

"Could be, but we've got nothing else to go on. We'll get the report on the dirt from Barajas' feet tomorrow. Maybe we'll get lucky. In the mean time, we've got some interviews to finish and I want to check around the area again. Might be something we missed the first time."

"Okay. Keep me posted. I'll be in a meeting upstairs most of the day tomorrow, but come and get me if anything major breaks. Vince, what does your gut tell you about this one?"

Vince was quiet for a moment. "I'm beginning to think this may be a revenge killing, Boss. Maybe not against Barajas personally, but against scum like him. I think it's someone pissed at a system that let's guys like Barajas escape justice. I hope I'm not right about this, but my instincts seem to be leading me that way. Anyway, I've gotta go."

Vince left the office and drove to where Barajas' body had been found. He parked outside the alley, got out of the car and walked to the entrance. Standing there, he scanned the area, looking for anything that seemed out of place. He stood there for the next five minutes before walking in.

He walked slowly through the alley, searching the ground carefully for something, anything that looked like it didn't belong, that may have been missed by the evidence team. He knew he was missing something. The killer placed Barajas body there for a reason. He knew it would be found and Vince's instincts told him the killer would have left a sign. Vince was sure the cut on Barajas cheek *was* a one and there would be more murders to come.

He sat on an old plastic milk crate someone had left there and leaned against the wall, thinking, staring across the alley. He noticed something on the gray stucco across from him that didn't appear to belong. There was a piece of paper stuck to the wall, waving in the breeze. What was unusual was the fact that it was clean, not soiled or weather beaten, and appeared to be blank. It looked like someone had placed it there recently. In an instant he was on his feet moving across the alley. When he got to the wall he saw it was a clean sheet of paper with no writing or marks on it. Taking his pen from his pocket, he carefully lifted the paper and saw printing on the wall in white chalk. It was difficult to see on the light gray surface and he had to look closely to read it. It was just three words, neatly printed, that read,

"THE FIRST RETRIBUTION".

Chapter 6

The van from Atascadero State Hospital left San Francisco Juvenile Hall at 6:30 a.m. with Mitch Ballinger in the back. There was one Deputy and a psychiatric technician in the back and another Deputy driving. Entering the freeway, the driver drove south on Hwy 101 while the technician poured herself and the guard a cup of coffee from a large thermos. She poured one for the driver and handed it through the sliding steel grate in the wall that separated the driver from the passengers. Their young charge was handcuffed, had leg irons on, and was seat belted to the bench across from them. He did not speak or look up, keeping his gaze fixed on the bare floor of the van as they drove south out of the city. The guard and technician chatted quietly as they drove, sipping their coffee. The driver had tuned the radio to a local country and western station and had the volume loud enough so they could hear it in the back. There was not much traffic once they passed San Jose and continued south, going against the morning commute. The high fog had dissipated the further they went from San Francisco and the sun was shining brightly. As they approached Morgan Hill, traffic thinned even more until it seemed they were the only vehicle on the road. The technician dozed off while the guard read the latest issue of *People* magazine. Mitch had not spoken or moved since they began their journey.

The highway narrowed to two lanes in each direction as they drove past the town of Morgan Hill in the Santa Clara Valley. They continued south on the highway, and as the van rounded a curve, he passed a tow truck parked on the shoulder with its flashing yellow lights on. A short distance further on, the driver felt a slight bump as the van ran over something in the roadway.

The killer watched the van pass the spike strip he had placed on the highway. He got in the tow truck and drove along the shoulder a short distance and stopped. Getting out of the truck, he walked to the small spike strip and pulled it off the road, confident the van driver did not suspect his right front tire was losing air. He made his way to the stolen tow truck and threw the makeshift strip in the back. Getting in the driver's seat, he put the truck in gear, pulled it onto the highway and started driving after the van. From the tests he had done last week, he knew the van could go no further than a mile before the driver realized the tire was going flat. That would put them just past the little community of San Martin, a farming and livestock town just off the highway. The country was open, being mostly farms and ranches, and there was little traffic and no buildings or businesses open that could house troublesome witnesses. The perfect location for what he had in mind. Besides, what could be more normal than a tow truck stopping to help a motorist with a flat tire? He smiled to himself as he drove, seeing the van a half a mile up ahead. He tuned the radio to the oldies station as he sped up, slowly closing the distance.

After another half mile, he saw the van pulling off the highway onto the shoulder. As the van came to a stop, he continued past, to give them time to see their tire had gone flat and start to change it. He needed them to open the back of the van before arriving there and offering his help. He drove another two miles before finding the next off-ramp. He got off the highway, drove under the overpass and took the on ramp heading in the opposite direction, back toward the disabled van. As he passed it on the other side of the highway, he could see both deputies were out and the rear doors were standing open. He made a u-turn across the median a half-mile past them, and drove back to their location, pulling over behind their van. He got out and walked toward the deputies, a broad smile on his face.

***

Two hours later, Vince was sitting at his desk talking to the records division trying to find out if any officers made a traffic enforcement stop on a van or SUV in the few hours before Barajas body was found. The civilian clerk told him she would do a check and get back to him in an hour or so. Vince thanked her and hung up the phone, frustrated at the lack of clues and information he and the others had been able to find over the last four days. The press had printed a small article on page nine of the newspaper three days ago, and there was a brief mention of the killing on the local radio and TV stations before interest in the case waned. Another dead gang member did not generate much media interest.

"Hey, Clark," he called out, seeing his partner walking through the office, "any luck with that paper or the writing I found?"

"Nah. Had the crime lab check the paper for prints, but there were none. Guess our suspect wore gloves. They said the writing was done in chalk you could buy anywhere. There was nothing unusual about the writing either. I had our handwriting expert look at the photos and she said it would be impossible to do any kind of comparison with chalk writing. So far we're shit out of luck on this one, Vince."

"Seems that way, doesn't it, Mike," Vince said.

"Oh, yeah, you didn't get this yet. I just got the lab report an hour or so ago. The lab found the mud contained a high salt content, which means it came from somewhere near the waterfront. Also contained traces of creosote, so that means it was near a pier. They're continuing their analysis."

"Not much help there," Clark said. "All we've got here is shoreline and piers."

Vince stood up and stretched, then grabbed his empty coffee cup. "I've got the beat cops all along the Embarcadero, Fisherman's Wharf, China Basin, and Bayview-Hunter's Point on the lookout for anyplace that could be our elusive crime scene."

"What about the west shore, the Pacific side?"

"Not yet. I don't think our killer would go that far away. Since Barajas lived in the Hunter's Point area, that's where we should concentrate. We'll see what happens. Our best bet is that partial print. The boys are running it through our in-house records and the FBI fingerprint system."

At that moment Vince's phone rang. They looked at each other, then at the phone as it rang again.

"Don't answer that, Vince. Bound to be bad news," Clark said.

"Probably just records calling me back, you fool," Vince said, smiling as he picked up the phone. "Homicide, Torelli."

"Vince!" It was his boss, Lt. Simons. "Better get in here and listen to this."

"Listen to what?" he asked.

"This phone call I got holding. Look, just get your ass in here and bring Clark with you."

"We're on the way, Boss."

"What was that all about?" Clark asked.

"The boss wants us in his office, like now."

"Why? We do something wrong?"

"Nah. He's got a phone call he wants us to listen in on. We better get in there. He sounded excited about something."

Vince knocked on Simons' door and was waved into the office. Lieutenant Simons, talking on the phone, motioned for them to close the door and sit down. Simons spoke into the phone, "And they found the van when? Ten a.m.? Okay, Okay, yeah, he's here now. I'll let him know. I'm sure he'll want to talk with you. All right, bye." Hanging up the phone Simons muttered, "Jesus H. Christ!"

"What's up, Boss?" Torelli asked.

"You know that kid who went on that shooting spree at his school a couple of months ago?"

"Yeah, I remember that," Clark said, leaning forward in his chair. "That was the 16-year-old who killed a teacher and a couple of students. He was found to be a nut case, wasn't he? Was being sent to the twinkie farm, right?"

"That's right. Too disturbed to stand trial. He was being transferred to Atascadero."

"So what's that got to do with us?" Vince asked, stifling a yawn.

"The Sheriff's van picked him up this morning about 6:30 and headed off to Atascadero. The van was found by the Highway Patrol parked on the shoulder along Route 101 in Santa Clara County around 10 a.m. with a flat tire. When the officer opened it up, he found the driver, guard and psych nurse bound and gagged. They had been sprayed with Mace. The kid was missing."

"You're not saying the kid did all of that by himself, are you?" Vince said, suddenly alert.

"Doesn't appear that way. That kid is a flake. He's not capable of pulling something like that off by himself. He either had help, or someone else did it."

"Someone else?" Vince said. "Someone snatched the kid?"

"It's possible."

"Someone else, like our killer?" Clark asked, sliding his chair closer to the desk.

"I don't know. That's why I called you two in here. The driver, guard, and tech have been taken to the hospital to be checked out, then will be taken to the Santa Clara Sheriff's Office in San Jose for their interviews. The lead detective said they won't get there for another hour, so that gives you time to get your butts down there and find out what you can. The van's been impounded, too, so you might want to take a look at it, see what you can find. Any questions?"

Vince smiled and said, "If it is our guy, there won't be any evidence. Maybe they got a look at him. We might get a description, though I got a feeling he's too careful for that. I'd be willing to bet he was wearing some sort of disguise."

"Maybe so, but even that is more than we got now. All right, get going. Report back to me when you get back."

"Right, Boss," Vince said as he and Clark stood up to leave.

Chapter 7

Forty five minutes later, they were buzzed into the investigations office at the Santa Clara County Sheriff's office. Sergeant Johnson, the lead investigator in the case briefed them as they walked down a hallway to the interview room where the van driver and the other deputy were waiting. They were uninjured, having been checked and cleared at the hospital. They suffered only some eye irritation from the Mace.

"You guys are welcome to sit in, but let us do the interview. Once we're done, you can have a go at 'em."

"Sure, Sergeant, it's your case. We don't even know if it's connected to ours," Vince said, looking at Clark. Before Clark could say anything Vince threw a quick glance at him and shook his head "no" as a warning to say nothing.

They walked into the small room. The driver of the van was seated at a small, grey, metal table in the middle of the room. Sergeant Johnson pulled out a chair from the table and sat across from him. "Is there anything we can get you before we begin?"

"Got any soda? I'm awful thirsty."

"No problem. Is Sprite okay?" The driver nodded and Johnson picked up the phone, asking someone to bring the soda to the interview room. Turning back to the driver, he said, "This interview is being video taped and recorded, so I'll need you to speak clearly and loud enough to be heard easily." Gesturing toward Torelli and Clark he said, "Meet Inspectors Torelli and Clark from San Francisco P.D. They'll be sitting in on the interview since your trip started out in SF. Let's get going by you stating your name and who you work for."

The driver clasped his hands together on the table and looked at Sergeant Johnson. Vince could see his eyes were very bloodshot from the Mace, though he did not seem to be suffering any lingering effects from it.

"My name is Stan Bishop and I am a deputy with the San Francisco County Sheriffs Office. I work in the transportation unit."

"As I understand it, Deputy Bishop, you were driving a van to Atascadero State Hospital, taking a 16-year-old by the name of Mitch Ballinger to the hospital per the court order. Who was with you?"

"Deputy Oscar Rojas, who was the guard in the back of the van, and a psych technician from the hospital, Angie Dexter."

"Isn't it unusual for a hospital technician to be with you during one of these transfers?" Johnson asked.

"Yeah. Usually it's just me and a guard or two, depending on who the prisoner is. She came along because of the kid's age."

"So, tell us what happened when you got to Morgan Hill."

"Well, everything was goin' along fine. No problems at all. We had been traveling for almost an hour and a half when I felt the van starting to pull to the right. We had just gone through Morgan Hill.

The further I went, the worst it got. I knew we were losing air outta the front tire so I pulled off the highway and got out to see what was up. The right front tire was flat."

"Could you see what caused the flat?"

"Nah. I didn't look. All I was thinking about was having to change the tire myself."

"Couldn't you call your office and have them send another van, or someone to fix it?" Sergeant Johnson asked, scribbling some notes on a pad of paper he had in front of him.

"Yeah, but it would have taken at least an hour and a half for someone to get there. The kid was no problem, what with both me and Oscar there, and I could change the tire myself in ten minutes and be long gone by then."

"What happened next?"

"I told Oscar what the problem was and what I was going to do. He said it should be okay, as the kid hadn't moved or said anything since we set out. Besides, the kid was handcuffed, had leg irons on, and was shackled to the seat. I had Oscar get the jack outta the back for me while I got the spare from under the van. That's when the tow truck drove up."

"Did you see what company it was from?"

"Didn't have any markings on it. The driver pulled up behind us and got out. Asked me if I needed some help."

Vince cut him off, saying, "Hold on a second. Can you give us a better description of the tow truck?"

Sergeant Johnson shot a look at him, turned back to Deputy Bishop and said, "Yeah, can you?"

"Yeah. It was mostly yellow, at least the cab was yellow. The bed was dark red, and the tow equipment was painted black. No markings and no company name."

Vince turned to Sergeant Johnson. "Do you have an APB out on the truck?"

"Yeah. Think it was stolen?"

"You can count on it. I'd bet you'll find it within a few miles of the van, too, if it's what I think it is."

"What's that?" Johnson asked.

"Not yet. I don't want to speculate at this time. Not until I have more information."

"Suit yourself." Sergeant Johnson turned back to the driver. "Go ahead, Deputy, what happened next?"

"The guy, you know, the tow driver, came walking up with this goofy grin on his face. Asked if he could help. Oscar and I both were outta the van, standing at the back when this guy suddenly brings his hand up from his side and sprays us with Mace. Same time he's doing that, he pulls a gun from behind him with his other hand and starts shouting for us to get on the ground. Me and Oscar, we couldn't see nuthin', our noses were runnin' and eyes burnin'. I thought about trying to draw my weapon, but I knew I'd be a dead man if I did, so I just laid on the ground, face down. Oscar must've done the same thing, cause the guy says, 'You two stay that way and no one gets hurt.' Then I hear him tell Miss Dexter to get outta the van. Next thing I know, sounds like she's on the ground, too, and the guy takes my gun from my holster, then tells me to put my hands behind my back. When I did, he puts the tape around my wrists, and puts a strip over my eyes and puts a couple'a wraps around my mouth. I found out later he did the same to Oscar and Miss Dexter."

"How long did all this take?" Sergeant Johnson asked.

"I dunno. Maybe two or three minutes. This guy knew what he was doing. Once he taped us up, he took us one at a time to the van and made us get in. I still couldn't see anything 'cause of the pepper spray. He had a gun pressed to the side of my neck, so I wasn't about to argue with him."

There was a soft knock on the door and a young deputy came in with a can of Sprite, which he placed on the table, then left.

Sergeant Johnson said, "Go on, Deputy."

"After he put us in the van, he pulled my keys off my belt. I heard chains rattling a short time later, and figured he must have unlocked the kid. Next thing I know, the back doors of the van slam shut and he was gone, and as I found out later, he took the kid with him."

"Can you describe him any better than what you gave the deputies at the scene?"

The driver picked up the cold can of soda, opened it and took a long drink before answering. "Man, that hits the spot," he said. "I been thinking on that. I already told them what he looked like, but now I seem to remember somethin' odd about him."

"Like what?" Vince asked. "A scar, did he limp, what?"

"No, nuthin' like that. His face was, like, just ordinary looking, you know? I didn't even get a good look at him."

"How about his height, or weight?"

"Well, best as I can recall, he seemed about my height, five nine or so, stocky, though it was hard to tell his weight because of the coveralls he wore."

"Moustache or beard? Unshaven?" Clark asked, leaning over the table toward the driver.

"No, but there was something odd about him."

"What?" Vince asked him. "Think hard, Deputy, this could be important."

"Damn. It's hard to remember, it happened so fast. Wait. I know, his skin looked pasty white, like he had makeup on, and his hair. It looked like something out of the 50's."

"The 50's? How so?" Vince asked.

"You know, the greaser look. Black, slicked back, long sideburns, duck tailed, a curl in the front. Looked like Elvis hair."

"Elvis hair," Vince muttered, shaking his head.

"Yeah. Elvis hair."

Sergeant Johnson stood up and stretched, then asked, "Anything else you remember?"

"Nah. The rest of the stuff I gave to the deputy at the hospital."

"Okay, then. I got nothing more," Johnson said, looking at Vince and Clark. "You guys got any questions?"

"Just a couple," Vince said, leaning back in his chair. "You said the suspect ordered you to the ground. How did he do that, or actually, what did he say? I need you to try to remember his exact words."

"Well, let's see. Right after he sprayed us and pulled the gun, he started yelling 'get on the ground, get on the ground'. Once I got down he yelled, 'face down, arms and legs spread', then, 'Make it so'."

"Could you tell where he was standing when he did this?" Vince asked, sitting up and leaning forward. He shot a quick glance at Clark.

"Sounded like he had moved behind me, but I can't be sure. Everything was happening so fast."

"Alright Deputy, you've been a big help."

Sergeant Johnson said, "That will do it for now, Deputy Bishop. We'll get in touch with you if we have any more questions. Why don't you call it a day, go home and relax? Be back in my office at 8 a.m. tomorrow and we'll go over your statement."

"Thanks, Sarge," Bishop said, standing up. He turned to Vince and Clark. "See ya later."

After he left, Vince turned to Sergeant Johnson. "It sounds like the suspect knows a bit about police procedure. Sounded to me like he was doing a felony take down, from the words he used and the way he handled his weapon and Mace."

Sergeant Johnson agreed. "Yeah, it does. But why the hairdo and makeup? Was it just a disguise?"

Clark stood up and walked over to the window. "He was drawing attention away from his face. That, plus the makeup. There's no other explanation, and it worked."

"I think you're right, Mike," Vince said. "He wears an Elvis wig and makeup and that's all the witnesses will remember, the most prominent features. Very smart of him. This gets stranger and stranger the more we learn. And what he said to the deputies, the 'make it so'. It rings a bell but I can't remember where I heard it before."

The phone rang and Sergeant Johnson walked over to the table. "Johnson," he said, then was quiet while he listened, every once in a while saying, "Is that so?" and "No shit!"

After he hung up, he looked at Vince and Clark. "You ain't gonna believe this. My partner just called from the impound yard. He was supervising the forensics on the van and you know what he found? The flat tire was caused by a spike strip! He found a couple of the spikes still imbedded in it."

Vince looked up. "How can that be? The driver said his tire went flat gradually, not quickly like it would from a spike strip."

"He said he had the crime scene tech pull one out and it was very small, much smaller than a commercially made product, the kind law enforcement uses. That would account for the slower leak. It would feel more like a regular flat."

"Yeah, I guess it would. So that means it was home-made. Man, this guy is clever! He really plans these out."

"You talk like he's done this before," Sergeant Johnson said. "What aren't you telling me?"

Vince turned to him. "We had a homicide in the City last week and I think it's the same suspect."

"Why?" Johnson said, sitting down at the table.

"It seemed at the time to be a revenge killing, but now I think it's more a vigilante type murder. The victim in our case was responsible for the death of a three-year old child in a drive-by shooting, but the D.A. was unable to prosecute him because the only witness disappeared. We found the shooter a few days later in an alley, cut up like yesterday's fish. Now this kid gets taken. Has to be the same guy."

"Are you sure?" Johnson asked.

"Not positively, but the kid goes and shoots up his school, kills four people, then is ruled mentally incompetent to stand trial and gets sent to Atascadero. I'm thinking our suspect sees it as failed justice, so he kidnaps him to dispense his own special kind of punishment. I'm willing to bet the kid turns up dead in the next day or so."

"Unless you find him first," Johnson said.

"We won't. Listen, Sergeant, if you learn anything else of interest, let us know. I'll keep you posted on our end as well. The killer has only struck in San Francisco, but that doesn't mean he won't branch out if he finds a likely target somewhere else. Keep an eye out for any disappearances of ex-cons or anyone who may fit the victim profile."

"I will. Be talking with you."

***

On the drive back to San Francisco, Vince thought about what the deputy had told him. He was certain it was the same suspect as in Barajas murder, and he knew the boy's body would turn up in a day or two.

"Back to the basics, eh, Vince?" Clark said, as he maneuvered through traffic.

"Yep. Unless we get really lucky, that's the only way we're gonna solve this one."

"I got to say, this guy is really clever. He planned this out to last detail," Clark said, with a half smile. "This is gonna be a tough one to solve, Vince. Hardly any evidence at the scene, no good description of the suspect, no murder location, and, so far, no body. I called the County forensics guys, but there was nothing of evidentiary value left in the tow truck or the van. They got the tape the killer used to bind the deputies and the woman, but there were no prints on it. I suppose we could match it to the role it was torn from if we ever find that, but I don't think that's going to happen. It's getting real frustrating, dealing with this guy."

"I know, Mike. All we can do is keep plugging along. He has to make a mistake sometime, and I hope it's sooner than later. When he does, he's ours."

Chapter 8

In the city, Vince drove slowly along the shoreline south of Market Street. He avoided the area north of Market, as it was clogged with tourists visiting Fisherman's Wharf, Ghirardelli Square, and the host of other locations and activities that made San Francisco one of the most popular tourist attractions in the world. The wharves north of Market Street were newer and had been refurbished in the last few years, and Vince felt the killer would not chance using one of them. There was too much activity in the area and too many potential witnesses.

South of Market was a different story. In the last few years, they had become more and more run down, and several had been abandoned. The piers had rotted and the wharves were sagging from neglect.

He parked under the Bay Bridge, and walked down the Embarcadero past several of the old wharfs, all the way to China Basin, peering into the abandoned buildings and questioning those people he met along the way. He was unable to see inside most of the rundown buildings because of the dirt and dust coating the windows, and all the doors he tried were either locked or chained shut. There were chain link and barbed wire fences surrounding the abandoned warehouses. After two hours he had found nothing of value and no one was able to provide him with any new information that could help him find the killer. Vince sighed with frustration and decided to call it a night.

***

Back at his office, he unlocked his desk and pulled the Ballinger file from the drawer. He began to read it for the twentieth time, hoping to see something he had missed.

After another hour of fruitless study, he put the file back in the drawer, locked the desk, got up and stretched, then headed out of the building to the parking lot. He thought he would make one pass by the school where the shootings took place, then head home.

He drove to Masterson High School and parked on the street out front. He sat in the car for a few minutes, trying to imagine the shootings at the school, looking around the area. There was nothing going on at the school and the gates to the parking lots were locked. There were few cars parked on the street and just a single vehicle, a white van, moving slowly up the street toward him. He paid no attention to the van as he got out of his car and crossed the street.

As he stepped up onto the sidewalk, he stopped, and turned around. He had the uncanny feeling that he was being watched. It was nothing more than a feeling, but Vince had learned to trust his instincts. The feeling of danger was strong, so strong that he pushed his coat back and unsnapped his holster. With his hand gripping the butt of the pistol, he looked up and down the street. He could see no one in the area, and the only thing moving was the white van, driving a bit below the speed limit as it moved past him.

He stood there another ten seconds, carefully looking around, until the feeling passed. An involuntary shudder passed through him.

He took a deep breath, and thought, *getting nervous in your old age, eh, Vince?* then snapped his holster shut and pulled his coat over the weapon. He turned back to school and walked into the schoolyard.

As he turned the corner and drove slowly past the school, the killer was shocked to see Inspector Torelli crossing the street ahead of him. A momentary wave of panic engulfed him and set his mind to racing, wondering how Torelli came to be here at this particular moment. He looked around wildly, searching for the other cops he knew had to be lurking behind parked cars and bushes, waiting for him to drive into their trap so they could rush out and surround him, pointing their automatic weapons and pistols at him, hoping for him to make one false move so they could kill him. Well, he would not give up meekly, no sir, not him. They would get more than they bargained for.

He reached into the center console and pulled out the .40 caliber Smith and Wesson semi-auto pistol, almost dropping it because his hand was so sweaty. Thumbing off the safety, he held it alongside his leg as he took a couple of deep breaths and continued driving slowly down the street.

Inspector Torelli crossed in front of him, paying no attention to him or the van. Torelli kept walking as he drove past, approaching the schoolyard gate. He looked in his side view mirror as he drove, seeing

Torelli stop on the sidewalk, turn around and look right at him. After a few seconds, he saw him turn back around and disappear from view as he walked around the corner of the building. He realized there were no other cops hiding along the street, and no one rushed out toward him. He held his breath until he got to the corner and turned right, then exhaled slowly.

He took a deep breath, and began to chuckle to himself. How foolish he felt. There was no way this was anything more than just a coincidence. He was too smart for them. They couldn't compete with his superior intellect. He felt much calmer now that he realized the truth. He put the pistol back in the consol, then turned the radio up and began happily singing along to the oldies. As he drove, he couldn't help glancing into the rear view mirror every now and then, just to reassure himself.

***

Vince walked around the corner of the building, heading toward the student quad area. He didn't know why he felt the need to come here or what he was looking for, but he knew he had to come. He walked into the quad and saw it was empty except for one person sitting on bench with his back to him, leaning against a tree.

He looked up at the sound of birds chirping, seeing a small flock of sparrows flying through the clear blue sky. Looking around the quad again, he could see nothing out of the ordinary except the person on the bench. He had not moved in the last few minutes. Vince walked toward him, becoming more concerned the closer he got. He walked faster, then broke into a trot.

As he ran around the bench, he was shocked to see the person was a young teenage boy. His shirt was open to the waist and his chest was covered with blood. His face had several deep cuts on it, and the half dried blood dripped slowly from his chin. His eyes stared dully at nothing, the spark gone. Vince knelt by the body and felt for a carotid pulse, knowing he would find none. He could see the long, deep cuts on his chest and knew he was dead. Looking closely at his face, he saw what appeared to be the number "2" carved on his right cheek. His heart raced as he drew his weapon and looked around, checking to see if the suspect was still in the area. He could see there was no one else around and turned back to the body. *Mitch Ballinger,* he thought. *Poor bastard.*

Vince walked around Ballinger's body, carefully looking for the chalk writing he knew he would find, and there it was, written on the bench next to the body, "The Second Retribution". What shocked him even more was the small printing under it that said, "More to come."

"God Damn it. Shit!" he shouted to the empty quad. He sat on the bench next to the body, pulled his cell phone out of his pocket and dialed his office. When his call was answered, he said, "I just found Mitch Ballinger's body."

Chapter 9

Monday dawned bright and clear in the east bay, but San Francisco was blanketed in its customary fog and damp drizzle, which would burn off by noon, resulting in a sunny, though windy day. As Vince drove over the Bay Bridge, he turned his wipers on. He thought about finding Ballinger's body two days earlier. He knew he had to have just missed the killer. The body was still too fresh to have been on the bench for long, and he couldn't shake the memory of feeling he was being watched at the school. He remembered the white van driving slowly down the street, and wondered if it was the killer's van.

Vince arrived at the Coroners Office by 7:30. Parking near the side door, he got out of the car, locked the doors and walked up to the door. He knocked loudly several times, peering through the frosted glass until he saw a figure approaching. The lock snapped and the door opened, and Dr. Chamberlin motioned him in.

"About time, Vince. I've been here for two hours already, and you, who was in such an all-fired rush to have the autopsy done, show up late!"

"Aw, c'mon, Doc. Gimme a break. You know I didn't need to be here during the procedure. All I need is to find out what you found, not how you found it. Besides, autopsies give me the willies."

"Oh, sure. The big war vet, homicide inspector can't stand the sight of a little blood? Don't give me that, Torelli. I've known you too long."

"I was up late last night working on this and overslept a bit. Do you still love me?"

"I don't know why, but yes, I do. Give us a kiss, will ya?"

"Forget it, Doc, I'm a happily married man. So, what can you tell me about this one?"

"Had to have been done by the same suspect, Vince. But I think you already knew that. The cuts are the same, in the same approximate locations. They're pretty much the same depth and length as the cuts on Barajas. If nothing else, your killer is consistent."

"You found the '2' carved on his cheek?"

"Yep. Same as the other victim. Not deep, but carefully done so there could be no mistake as to what it was. But why write on the bench, too? He must know we would link the two homicides."

"Yeah, Doc, he would. If you ask me, he's teasing us. The police, I mean. I think by writing 'more to come' he's letting us know he isn't finished yet, and that he's smarter than the police. Kind of a 'catch me if you can' thing. Almost as if he is matching wits with us, fully expecting to come out on top. I think he will get bolder and bolder, and if he does, he will start making mistakes. Then, I will find him."

"That you will, Vince. Just don't get so wrapped up in the chase you get careless."

"Thanks for your concern, Doc, but don't worry."

"By the way, forensics found some traces of creosote on the victim's shoes. Some mud traces, too, with a high salt content. Same murder location?"

"I'd be willing to bet on it. You said it before, Doc. He is consistent, and that's gonna be his downfall."

"I hope you're right. The measurements of the wounds, in particular the fatal stab wound to the heart, indicate a strong possibility the same weapon was used as in the other murder. If not the same weapon, it's one very close to it."

"Thanks, Doc. That's good to know. Did the crime lab fingerprint the body?"

"Yep. Nothing. They're convinced the killer wore gloves. They also vacuumed him, including his hair. Clean as a whistle. They took his clothing with them for further study. We took a blood sample and the lab is testing it for drugs or alcohol, but I don't think they will find anything."

"Any bruises on Ballinger's body? On his head, in particular."

"No, nothing. Why do you ask?

"Just covering the bases, Doc. Now, I gotta get to the office. Simons will be wanting an update. If you turn anything else up, let me know first, Okay?"

Doctor Chamberlin looked puzzled for a moment, then shrugged. "As you wish, Vince. You want to tell me why?"

"Not yet, Doc. Just a hunch I have."

"Okay, Torelli, your wish is my command."

"Thanks. See ya, Doc," Vince said, and closed the door behind him.

***

An hour later, Vince was sitting in Lieutenant Simon's office as the Lieutenant waved a newspaper over his head, pacing back and forth in his office, shouting at Vince and his partner. His morning coffee had grown cold sitting in his cup on his desk

"Look at this headline," he shouted. "Front page! How the hell did they get that much information, huh? Front page, God dammit! Now the Chief wants to see me, and he's gonna be asking me these same questions."

He stopped his pacing, facing Vince and Mike. "Don't just sit there. Say something! How did they know about the number two carved on his face? And they knew the exact wording of the message on the bench! They knew about the other homicide, that the same message was written on the alley wall. They surmised, rightly, that the same suspect is involved. They're calling him the 'Retribution Killer'. How, in God's name, did they know, Torelli? You have anything to do with this?"

"You know I didn't," Vince said, hoping to calm his boss down. "This is not good for your blood pressure, .L.T."

"The hell with that! Don't change the subject!" he hollered, throwing the paper on his desk. He sat heavily in his chair, took out his handkerchief and mopped the sweat from his face. Picking up the paper once more he said, in a more conversational tone, "Let's read some of the article, shall we? 'San Francisco Police today refused to confirm or deny the two homicides are related. This reporter has obtained information from a source close to the investigation that both the victims were killed in the same manner and that both had a number carved on their face. There was a similar message written in chalk left near each of the bodies. Sources indicated the murders were done as retribution for the victim's unpunished crimes.' Did you hear that, boys? A source CLOSE to the investigation! As far as I know, there are really only two people close to the investigation, AND I'M LOOKING AT BOTH OF THEM!"

"C'mon, Boss," Clark said. "We're not the leak."

"Either one of you know this reporter, this, what's her name, Liz Maltby?"

Vince groaned inwardly. "Yeah, I met her a couple of times on other cases. You remember the case I had last year involving the murder of the professor from San Francisco State? Turned out he was pimping his female students? She was the reporter who got the information that broke the case when one of the girls came to her. We spent some time together on that one."

"No kidding! Now why doesn't that surprise me? Listen," he said. "I know you guys didn't leak this info. What I need is for you to stop the leak. Vince, you keep the report under wraps. I don't want anyone not involved in the investigation reading it, and you decide who gets to see it on a need to know basis, got it?"

"Got it, Boss," Vince said.

"Oh, yeah, I almost forgot. You guys are getting an Assistant D.A. assigned to you. He'll help with the legalities of the investigation should you need a search warrant or whatever. Expect him sometime this afternoon."

"Aw 'mon, L.T. He's just gonna get in the way," Vince moaned.

"Learn to live with it, Torelli. You're to keep him informed of the progress of this investigation. He is to assist you with the case. He's been assigned as part of the task force. If anything breaks, he is to be included, even called if it happens after hours. In other words, he is your shadow, understand?"

Vince and Clark started to protest when Lieutenant Simons bellowed, "I don't want to hear it! This conversation is over. I've gotta go see the Chief."

***

Later that day Vince was at his desk, talking with the San Jose investigators, when a shadow fell over him. He looked up and saw a young looking man, dressed in an ill-fitting brown suit, and wearing wire-rim glasses grinning at him.

"Listen, Sgt. Johnson, I've got a visitor. Fax me that stuff, okay? Yeah, that's the number. All right, I'll call you later." He hung up the phone, turned to the stranger and said, "Can I help you?"

"Are you Inspector Torellli or Inspector Clark?" the man asked, looking at a small post-it attached to the file folder he carried.

"Let me guess. You're the ADA assigned to the homicides, right?"

"Right. I'm Robert Cullin. You can call me Robbie," he said. Placing the file folder on the desk, he stuck out his right hand while pushing his glasses up on his nose with his left. Looking around the office, he said, "This is really neat! I'm actually in the homicide office! Never been here before, and now I get to work here!"

Vince grasped his hand, trying not to grimace at how clammy it felt. After a weak single shake, Robbie dropped Vince's hand like it was on fire. "I'm Torelli," Vince said, motioning Clark to come over, and when he did, said, "Meet Robbie Cullin from the D.A.'s office. He's gonna be helping us with the case. Robbie, meet Inspector Clark."

"Hey, Robbie, how ya doing?" Clark asked, shaking his hand.

"Okay, Mike," Cullin said. Looking around the room, he said to Vince, "So, where's my desk? And I'll need my own phone line and computer."

"Wait a minute, Cullin."

"Robbie."

"Alright, Robbie. Look at that door over there, the one with the number 450 on it. See what it says? Can you find anything that even remotely says this is the D.A.'s office?"

"Of course not. This is the homicide investigations office."

"That's right. Now, you've never been here before and never worked with any of us, so there will be no desk, no phone, and no computer. You can pull up a chair by either Clark's or my desk, and you can use our phones, but don't use the computers unless you check with us first. You are here to assist in the investigation, to make sure there will be no legal slip-ups should we find this guy, and that is it."

"Okay, Inspector Torelli. I'm sorry. I am well aware of what my duties are. I apologize if I came on a bit strong, but I'm just anxious to get going. I can be a help to you. I have lots of contacts at City Hall, so if you need things expedited, I can get it done. And I just found out I was working here yesterday. All I knew was I was to report to Inspector Torelli."

"Good. I appreciate that," Vince said. He leaned back in his chair and took a deep breath. He looked at Deputy D.A. Cullin, who was looking at the floor, shuffling his feet. "Look, Robbie, I apologize if I sounded gruff, but there's a lot of pressure being exerted on this investigation. Now, on top of investigating the homicide, I have to find out who is leaking info to the press. What d'ya say we start all over?"

"Okay by me, Vince...I can call you Vince, right?"

"Sure. Now, here's the case files if you want to review them. Let me know if anything jumps out at you."

"All right."

ADA Cullin pulled a chair up to Vince's desk and sat down. He opened the report file and began reading. Vince used the opportunity to take a closer look at him. He had thin, mousy brown hair, with a bald spot on the top. He had let it grow long on the side and combed it over to cover his baldness. He was short, a bit pudgy, and looked soft.

Vince slid his chair back from the desk and stood up. "Hey, Robbie. I gotta go. My son is playing in his soccer championships tonight." He handed Robbie one of his cards. "If anything comes up, call me. My home number is on the back, but try my cell phone first. Clark will be here for a while, so when you finish with that file, give it to him. He can answer any of your questions."

"Okay, Vince. Here, take one of my cards," Cullin said, scribbling on the back as he talked. "My home number is on the back."

"All right." Turning the card over, Vince noted the handwritten number on the back. "This is a local number. You live here in the city?"

"Yeah. I see by your area code you live in the East Bay."

"Yes. Great place to live, but a bitch of a commute everyday. Look, I better get going, so I'll see you Monday morning, 8 a.m."

"Hey, have a great weekend."

"You, too." Vince turned to Clark. "Mike, call me tomorrow."

"I will, Vince. Good luck to Tony tonight."

"Thanks, I'll let him know."

Chapter 10

Vince woke with a start, breathing hard and sweating profusely. The nightmare was particularly clear tonight. He had dreamt he was back on the airbase in Vietnam during the '68 Tet attack. He rubbed his shoulder, relieved to find it was not bleeding. The bullet scar on his leg ached. He remembered the explosion that blew him out of his jeep, heard the gunfire, felt the fear, saw his partner fall, gravely wounded.

He sat up, looking at the clock on his nightstand, seeing it was 3:47 in the morning. Leaning back against the headboard, he closed his eyes and took a few deep breaths, trying to slow his pounding heart.

"The dream again, honey?" his wife said, rolling over and looking at him.

"Sorry, babe. Didn't mean to wake you."

"Look at you. You're sweating up a storm. Must have been bad tonight. You all right?"

"Yeah. It's been awhile since the last one." He unconsciously rubbed the bullet scar on his leg.

"How about I make us some coffee?" Maggie said, pushing the covers off and sitting up.

"Thanks." His breathing had slowed and his heart was no longer pounding. He knew he would not be able to get back to sleep. He got out of bed, went to the bathroom and splashed some water on his face, then went to the kitchen where Maggie was making the coffee.

"Want to talk about it?" she asked, sitting down.

Vince sat across from her. "Same dream, Babe. I'm back at the airbase during the attack and I feel so helpless. In the dream, no matter what I do, I can't find a safe place. They just keep coming, and no matter how many I kill, they never stop." He ran his fingers through his hair and took a deep breath. "You know what really pisses me off? I know it's only a dream and I should be over it by now."

"Don't be so hard on yourself, hon I don't think it's that easy to forget." She reached across the table and took his hand in hers. "Don't worry about it. That was something that will always be with you. It was such a huge part of your life, and you probably will have these dreams the rest of your life. But, one good thing, they seem to be getting more and more infrequent. It's something we have to live with."

"I know. I called Sanders yesterday just to see how he's doing. Maybe that's what caused the dream to come back."

"Maybe. Talking with him could have triggered it. You told me you saw him get shot and thought he had been killed."

"Yeah, you're probably right. That was the worst night of my life, when I thought he was dead. I guess I'll never get over it."

Maggie came around the table and took him in her arms. Pulling his head against her chest, she gently stroked his cheek. "You don't have to. Don't try, babe, just accept that it will always be a part of you, Okay?"

Vince looked up at her and smiled. "How do you always know the right thing to say to me?"

"I love you, that's why."

They talked until after five, drinking their coffee. Maggie went back to bed, while Vince got dressed and went for a run.

Chapter 11

Vince arrived at his desk at 7:15 Monday morning, before Clark or ADA Cullin showed up. He pulled a business card from his card file and, after checking to make sure no one was in earshot, dialed the number.

"San Francisco Chronicle, Liz Maltby speaking."

"Liz, it's Vince Torelli."

"Ah, the elusive Inspector Torelli, the one who won't return my phone calls. To what do I owe this honor?"

"We need to meet. I want to talk, maybe share some information?"

"So, that answers my question. You need something and are willing to trade, huh? So talk. What's on your mind?"

"Not on the phone. How about I buy you lunch at Alioto's, at the wharf?"

"Wow! This must be something really important. Okay, big spender. Twelve-thirty okay with you?"

"See you then," he said, then quickly hung up as Clark walked toward him.

***

An hour later Vince, Clark, Cullin, and Lt. Simons were in the Lieutenant's office reviewing the progress of the investigation.

"So," Lt. Simons said, "we don't have squat on this guy. How can there be nothing?"

"We're missing something, Boss. Nobody leaves no clues. There's always something left behind. We just haven't found it yet," Vince said.

Cullin said, "I don't see what it could be, Vince. No prints, no foreign hair or fibers on the victims matched with any cases somewhere else in the Bay Area. No murder scene. What's left?"

"I don't know, not yet, but there is always something. He'll make a mistake and we'll find him, of that I am sure."

"Well, you ain't gonna do it sitting here," Lt. Simons growled. "Get back to work."

Vince spent the rest of the morning working on the computer, trying to see if this case matched with a case somewhere else in the country. He also made several calls to the forensics lab, asking if they had found anything new on the body or at the scene. There was nothing to add to what he already knew.

When he looked at his watch, he saw it was 11:45. He grabbed his coat, walked to Lieutenant Simon's office, and told him he was going to lunch. He arrived at the restaurant early and selected a table from which he could watch the door. He did not want to be seen with the reporter, especially now that she had broken the story, citing "sources close to the investigation". He ordered coffee and sipped it slowly, waiting for the reporter to show up. He saw her walk in a few minutes late, and approach the hostess. When she looked in his direction, he waved her over.

"Nice to see you, Inspector," Liz said as she sat across from him.

Liz Maltby was in her early 30's, and real ambitious. She was not afraid to make deals and promises she had no intention of honoring, and she used her looks and charm, which could be considerable when she wanted them to be, to get what she wanted. She was not used to being told no. She stood 5'7", and had a trim, athletic figure, brown hair with reddish highlights, and blue eyes. Her hair was shoulder length and fashionably styled, and she used little makeup. She wore no nonsense business attire that fit her hard charging attitude.

The first time she had noticed the handsome young inspector at the police department, she asked the receptionist about him. She was interested in getting to know him better, and it did not matter to her that he was married. She began showing up at his crime scenes, and arranging "chance" meetings. The more she saw him, the more she was attracted to him.

Her chance came a couple of years later when a professor from San Francisco State College was found savagely murdered on campus. Vince had been transferred to the homicide division, and was the lead investigator. The case was particularly difficult right from the beginning, as there were few clues, and no apparent motive for his murder. Vince did an extensive background check on the victim and could find no logical reason why he would be murdered. He interviewed the family, his colleagues at San Francisco State, and most of his students without finding anything that could lead to why the professor had been murdered.

After a week had passed and Vince was no closer to solving the case, he got a call from Liz asking to meet. She said she might have some information that could help in the investigation.

"I'm awfully busy, Miss Maltby. Can you tell me over the phone?"

"Well, I could, but I won't. It will cost you a dinner, Inspector."

"Look, Liz, I don't have time for this. How about meeting me here, or I can come by your office?"

"Nope. Meet me at seven thirty tonight at O'Bannion's on Market Street. Otherwise, you get nothing. You know where it is?"

"Yes. How do I know what you have is worth it?"

"Why, Inspector, I'm hurt! And a little insulted. Trust me, Torelli, it's worth it, so you need to meet me. That's the way I want it, and that's the way it's got to be."

"Alright, Liz, alright. I'll meet you. Seven thirty?"

"Seven thirty it is."

Vince hung up the phone and cursed under his breath. He called Maggie and told her he would be late, that he had some work to catch up on. He hated lying to her, but felt it was not a good idea to tell her about Liz, at least not yet.

Vince thought about what Liz had hinted. *What does she know?* He wondered, *and what does she want for the information?* Vince was well aware of the talk about her around the Hall of Justice, how she couldn't be trusted and that her word was worthless. Never the less, he decided to meet her to see what she had to offer.

While interviewing the professor's students, Vince had gotten the feeling that some of them were holding back information. Try as he would, he couldn't get them to admit it, but his instincts told him he didn't know the full story of the professor. He knew Liz had also interviewed some of the murdered professor's students, and he wondered what she had uncovered that he hadn't.

He arrived ten minutes late and when he walked in, he could see Liz sitting in a corner booth toward the back, in the shadows. He walked over and slid into the booth, sitting across from her. "So, what's this all about, Liz?"

"Ooo, so business-like! Relax, Torelli. Dinner first, then we talk." Signaling the waiter, she said, "I've taken the liberty to order some wine. You do drink wine, don't you?"

"Hold on, Liz. I don't want to sound rude, but I really don't have time for this. If you have information for me, please tell me what it is. I, and the police department, will be extremely grateful, especially if it helps with the case."

She looked at him with a puzzled look on her face. "You just don't get it, do you, Torelli. This little soiree is more than just an information exchange."

She stopped talking as the waiter walked up with their wine. After he had poured them each a glass and left, she continued. "I guess there is only one way to say this, so, here goes." Liz reached across the table and covered Vince's hands with hers. "I want us to be friends, Vince."

"We are friends, Liz, aren't we?"

"Not like that. I want us to be *friends,* get it?"

"What are you saying, Liz?"

She sighed, shook her head and said, "Are you really that thick, Vince? I've been attracted to you from the first time I saw you. What I want is for us to be together. Wait!" she said, raising a hand, palm toward Vince. "Before you say anything, I know you're married. I don't care about that. I'm not interested in you leaving your wife. In fact, that's the one thing that will ruin it for me. All I want is for us to spend some time together once in a while. No commitments, Vince. Let's just have some fun."

Vince listened to her and when she paused, he pulled his hands from under hers and said, "So that's the price for the information? I gotta say, Liz, I never expected this. I'm very flattered, but I've got to tell you it will never happen."

"Why not, Vince?" she asked. "We could have a good time, no strings attached." Liz leaned back in the booth, one arm over the back, smiling at Vince. "I see us meeting once or twice a week. A little dinner, a little information exchange, and a little, well, I'm sure you get the picture."

Vince slid out of the booth and stood up. "Don't call me again, Liz, unless you want to give me the information you say you have, which I doubt is worth much anyway." Vince turned and walked out, his anger at her scheme apparent.

Ever since that time, Vince had avoided spending much time with Liz. He still would see her every so often, but hardly spoke to her other than when he had to as part of the job.

"So, Torelli, why did you want to see me?"

"Charming, as always, Liz. Shall we order first? The crab caesar here is excellent."

"Let's skip the pleasantries, Inspector. You said you had something to trade?"

"I'm still hungry, Liz, so, if you don't mind, I'm going to order lunch." Vince beckoned to the waiter and ordered the Caesar salad and a beer. Liz ordered a small dinner salad and a glass of Chardonnay. Vince waited until the waiter was out of earshot before talking.

"Before we get started, what we talk about is between you and me, not for publication. I know your reputation when it comes to keeping your word, and I am aware of the history between us, but in this case, you better keep it. If one word of what we talk about gets out, I will cut you out of the loop when we catch this guy, and I'll let your editors know about our deal and how you broke your word."

"When you catch him? Are you close?"

"No, but it's only a matter of time. You know me, too, Liz. I will find him, and if we work together, you'll get the exclusive scoop."

"That's what I like to hear, Vince. So, what do I have that you want?"

"You cited 'sources close to the investigation'. I need to know who those sources are."

Liz smiled. "You know I can't reveal that. You know what would happen if I did? No one would ever talk to me again, and there would go my career. Forget it, Torelli." She stood to leave. "I'm surprised you even asked."

"Now wait a minute, Liz. Don't get your panties in a bunch. I don't need names, I just need to know where the info came from. I need to know if the leak was from the police department, or somewhere else."

"Why is this so important, Vince?" she asked, sitting back down.

"Because whoever gave you that information knew things only two of us knew. Whoever contacted you either knows the killer, or is the killer."

"Oooh, how exciting!" She thought for a moment, then said, "Well, I'd like to help you, but the info came in by phone call. I only talked to the source."

"Was it a male or a female?'

"Listen, Vince. I'll tell you what you want to know, to a certain extent, but you can't tell anyone, either."

"Goes without saying. We both got a lot to lose if anyone finds out we've been talking."

"Okay. I'll trust you. It was a man, but he was disguising his voice. Had a cloth or something over the mouthpiece muffling his voice."

"What, exactly, did he say?"

"He asked if I wanted an exclusive on the retribution murders. I said I didn't have a clue what he was talking about, and he then told me about the homicides being related."

"Did he say how he knew that?"

"No. Only that he was close to the investigation and that the police were keeping the information from the media."

"What else did he say?"

"He said the police were baffled, had no evidence that would lead them to the killer, and that the killer was much cleverer than they were. He started rambling on about how the police wouldn't put much effort into the investigation because the victims deserved killing."

"Did he give any indication he was part of the investigating team?"

"No, but I got the feeling he knew a lot more than he was telling me."

"How? Was it something he said?"

"Yeah. I got the idea he was very close to the homicides, almost that he may have been the killer."

"I think he is. I think this guy has some sense of superiority, some Robin Hood complex. I think he believes what he is doing is justice, some misguided sense of righteousness. I think he will kill again, and again, and keep on killing until we catch him."

"What makes you think the caller was the killer?"

"Didn't he tell you about the numbers carved on the victim's faces? He also told you about the writing found where the victims were dumped, didn't he?"

"Well, yes, but couldn't anyone at the police department have gotten that information?"

"No, because only Clark and I and a few others knew that info. You know we always hold back some vital information only the killer would know. It helps eliminate the crank callers and identify legitimate calls. I know I didn't call you, and I'm certain Clark didn't. That leaves the killer." Vince paused, then said, "Wait a minute. There is one other who knew about the numbers cut into the victim's cheeks."

"Who, Vince?"

"Can't say just yet. Its something I'll have to look into before saying anything else."

"So what do we do from here? You need me and I need you. Can we form an alliance?"

"We're gonna have to. I need you to notify me immediately if you receive another call. Here's my personal cell number, and my home number," Vince said, handing her his business card with the numbers written on the back. "Call it anytime, night or day."

"All right. Here's my card with my numbers."

"Thanks, Liz. This is going to get a lot worse before it gets better. One more thing. You said the caller referred to the murders as the 'retribution murders'. Was that his exact words?"

"Yes. I thought it a good name, so that's why I used it in the article. Is it important?"

"I don't know. Here comes our food."

***

Torelli and Clark spent the rest of the day visiting police academies in the greater Bay Area, driving to the Alameda County Sheriff's Academy in Dublin, the Santa Rosa Academy, and the Napa Academy, interviewing the directors and going through the files of the recruits who either failed out or had been refused admission. They went through dozens of files with no luck. Vince planned their visits so that the last academy they visited was at Los Medanos College in Contra Costa County, a few miles from his home, again, finding nothing of interest.

"Let's call it a day, Mike. We're getting nowhere fast. Drop me at my house and take the car home. Will you have time to pick me up in the morning?"

"Sure. How does seven sound?"

"Sounds good. I'm gonna go over some of these files we got from the academies, see if anything jumps out at me."

"Want me to help?"

"Nah. I think this is a dead end. Just something we gotta do. Tomorrow, we'll visit our academy. I know the guy who runs it, so he'll give us what we need without a hassle."

As they pulled up to Vince's house, they could see his two sons kicking a soccer ball around.

"How are they doing with their soccer?" Clark asked.

"Good. Both have been recruited to play on club teams. Means a lot of traveling, though. How's Allie doing?"

"Pretty good. She's still a little young at 8, but seems to like the game."

"Sandy doing Okay?"

"Yeah. Started her fifth month and thinks she has gained way too much weight. I swear, she's driving me nuts. She's only gained 15 pounds."

Vince grinned and opened the car door. "The curse of the pregnant wife. Hang in there, partner. See you tomorrow."

As Vince walked around the front of the car, Clark leaned out the driver's window and said, "Yeah, easy for you to say. See ya in the morning."

Chapter 12

Charlie had a problem. Charlie liked to drink. In fact, because he liked to drink so much, he ended up in prison. Two and a half years earlier, Charlie left his favorite bar after a night of hard drinking and got in his car for the five-mile drive home. Two miles from his house, he ran a red light at fifty-three miles per hour, broadsiding a van that had entered the intersection from the cross street. Inside the van was a young father, his wife, and their two children, ages four and one and a half. The ensuing crash and fire killed them all.

Charlie, who suffered a broken leg and a few other minor injuries in the collision, was convicted of four counts of vehicular manslaughter and one count of felony drunk driving, and was sentenced to twelve years in prison on the manslaughter charges and six years on the felony drunk driving. He was remanded to the medium security facility at Vacaville. Since the judge ruled the sentences would run concurrent, he was paroled after two and a half years, free to pick up his life where he had left off. He never accepted responsibility for the crash, and never expressed any remorse. In spite of the objections of the District Attorney's Office and the families of his victims at his parole hearing, Charlie Sachs walked away from the state prison at Solano a free man.

He watched Sachs get off the bus, walk the short block to the apartment building and enter the front door. He had followed him from his job as a cook at an all night diner a few miles away. Parking across the street, he saw the lights go on in a second floor apartment a short time later. He got out of the car and walked across the street, then up the stairs to the front door. He read the name labels by the call buttons and saw Charlie Sachs' name next to the number 204. He smiled to himself, walked back to the car, and drove slowly away.

***

Vince and Clark arrived at the office after ten a.m., having met with the director of the Los Medanos police academy earlier, to find Cullin already hard at work, going through the missing person reports from the last few days.

"Morning, Robbie," Vince said, as he walked to the coffee maker and poured himself a cup. "You want some, Mike?" he asked.

"Not right now. Already had a couple of cups. You want me to continue trying to locate those academy rejects, Vince?"

"Yeah, see what you can do. There should only be a few left."

"I'll call our academy, too, and let them know what we're looking for. Holler if you need me."

"All right. What are you doing here so early, Robbie?"

"Checking the missing persons reports, like you suggested, Vince. Thought I could at least do that. Be of some help instead of just getting in the way."

"Thanks. That would be a help."

"Hey, Vince, I won't be back after lunch. Took the rest of the day off to attend the Star Trek Convention at Mosconi Center."

"Okay by me. I didn't know you were a Star Trek fan."

"Big time. Got every episode on video. I go to these conventions all over the place. Last year it was in Los Angeles. More than fifty thousand people attended it over the five days it ran. You ever watch it?"

"I used to watch the original series when I was in high school. Never got into the spin-offs, though."

"I got 'em all. And all the movies. You like the movies?"

"Yeah. Most of them were okay."

"Why don't you go with me? I get complimentary tickets. It will be fun."

"Thanks, but I'll pass. Got too much to do. Anything jump out at you with those missing person reports?"

"No. Routine stuff, mostly. A bunch of juveniles, couple of homeless types. Nothing else."

"Keep looking. Get hold of some of the larger departments in the bay area. Check their reports, too. I'm looking for people who have a record. If you come across anything like that, have them fax you a copy of the report and put it on my desk. Mike and I are gonna go interview a possible suspect in Napa, so we will be gone most of the day. If anything breaks, be sure to call me right away. I'll have my cell phone with me, and, in case you can't reach me, here's Clark's cell number. I'll see you tomorrow. Have fun at your conference."

"Thanks, Vince."

***

Torelli and Clark drove to Napa, and parked in front of a small apartment complex. They had decided to show up un-announced at the last known address of a recent drop-out from the police academy who had expressed some unorthodox feelings regarding the justice system. The academy director told them there had been some incidents involving what he called "excessive exuberance" by the cadet during the defensive tactics and un-armed combat training, resulting in another cadet sustaining a broken arm. The director said it was only the crowning event, that there had been other similar occurrences and that the cadet had been warned about his actions several times. Twice, he'd had to be taken home by his fellow cadets after too much drinking at a local club, narrowly avoiding a fight with the bouncers both times. He had been banned from the club, and the owner had contacted the Academy director to inform him of the two incidents.

Because of all of that, he was given the opportunity to resign from the academy, which he refused to do, necessitating his dismissal. The director said the cadet did not take it well, leaving the academy very agitated and angrily threatening revenge.

"Want to contact the manager first, Vince?" Clark asked, shutting off the engine.

"No. Let's just hit him up cold turkey. Last known address was here, apartment 21. Shall we?"

They walked up the stairs to number 21 and knocked on the door, standing off to one side while they waited for someone to answer. When no one answered, Vince knocked again, this time pounding harder on the door.

"What the hell's going on out here?"

Vince turned toward the voice and saw an elderly black man leaning out the window next door.

Vince pulled back his suit coat, showing the man his badge. "How ya doing, Sir? We're with the San Francisco Police Department. We're looking for Louis Machado. Have you seen him today?" Vince said, showing him the academy photo.

"Yeah, that's him all right. He don't live here no more."

"Oh, yeah? When did he move?"

"Las' month. Just up and disappeared. I say good riddance, too."

"Why would you say that? Was he not a good neighbor?"

"Ever since he got kicked outta the police school, he been raisin' hell around here, yellin' all the time 'bout how unfair it was, they was pickin' on him, how he was born to be a cop. Kept rantin' and ravin' about catchin' criminals. Said there was too many getting' away and somethin' needed to be done, always talkin' about how someone needed to take charge, how we needed to get back to dispensin' street justice. I was glad to hear he done left!"

Torelli and Clark exchanged looks, and Clark said, "Any idea where he might have gone?"

"Don't know for sure, but he always was talking about movin' to San Francisco. Said that was where the action was."

"Does he have any family in the area? Parents, brothers, sisters, cousins?" Clark asked.

"Beats me. Never talked with him too much. Never had any visitors that I saw."

"Anything else you can add? Anything at all?" Vince asked.

"Nope. Say, you never did say why you want to talk to him."

"Just had a couple of questions we need answered." Vince handed his business card to him. "If he comes back or shows up here, give me a call right away, okay?"

"Sure, Inspector."

"Thanks again. You've been a great help. Let's go, Mike."

Walking away from the apartment, Clark asked, "Now you want to contact the manager?"

"Yeah, yeah, yeah. You gonna rub it in?"

"Me? Why Vince, I'm hurt!"

"Uh huh. There's the office."

Vince flashed his badge again and asked the manager about Machado.

"The son of a bitch skipped out on his last month's rent!"

"So I guess that means he didn't leave a forwarding address?" Vince muttered.

"What?" the manager asked.

"Nothing. Take a look at this photo. Is that Louis Machado?"

"That's him."

"You know if he has any family in the area?"

"Nope. He wasn't too friendly. Never really talked too much."

Clark asked, "Do you have his rental agreement?"

"Yeah. I'll get it for you," he said, walking to a small desk in the corner of the office. He opened the bottom drawer and thumbed through the files. "That's funny. His file's not here! Now, that's odd."

"You sure it's gone?" Vince asked. "Maybe it's just misfiled."

"Shouldn't be. I filed it myself three months ago when he moved in. Nobody else messes with the files."

"Could somebody have gotten in there without you knowing?"

"It's possible. I never lock the office during the day, and I'm often gone, fixing things or working in the complex. Yes, I guess it would be pretty easy."

"Great," Vince said. "Well, thanks for the help. Call me if you see him or hear from him, okay?" Vince said, handing him a business card.

"Sure. Sorry I couldn't help out more."

"Don't worry about it."

They walked back to the car and once they got inside, Clark asked, "What now?"

"Maybe this is where Cullin can finally be some help," Vince said, pulling out his cell phone. He dialed his office number. "I hope he's still in the office."

"What can he do?" Clark asked, as he started the engine.

"He said he had lots of important contacts. let's see if he has one at the post office. Maybe he can get us a forwarding address. Hey, Robbie, it's Vince. Yeah, we're still in Napa. Listen, do you have any contacts at the post office? Good. I need you to see if you can locate a forwarding address for Louis Machado. Yeah, Machado, M-A-C-H-A-D-O. He's on the list of police academy rejects in the file. Can you do that before you leave today? Good. Call me if you find out anything. We're gonna be out in this area for awhile, then going to go to Harrigan's on Post Street for a couple of beers." "Does he know anyone who can help?" Clark asked.

"Maybe. Has a cousin who works in the Daly City post office. He's gonna call him and see if he can find out anything."

"What do you say we go back to the academy and contact the director?" Clark said. "Maybe he'll let us look in Machado's file. There's gotta be some family info in there, emergency contacts and such."

"Should be. Let's go, time's a-wasting."

***

Later that evening, Vince, Clark, and Cullin were sitting in a back booth, nursing their beers. Cullin had stopped by after the convention.

"This guy has got to be deranged," Vince said, taking a swig of his beer.

"Maybe not, Vince," Clark said. "Maybe he's just tired of the failures of our justice system. I know I am. You have expressed some doubts, too, you know."

"Yeah, I have, but we're not going around killing people because of it."

"Maybe he isn't, either," Cullin chimed in. "Maybe he has a different reason."

"Like what, Robbie?" Clark asked.

"Maybe he was a victim of a violent crime, or a family member was. Maybe he's just seeking revenge."

"Could be," Clark said, sipping from his beer bottle. "Personally, I find it a little hard to condemn the guy."

"What do you mean?" Vince asked.

"Well, look at who his victims are. They're all psychopathic killers who escaped justice somehow. I think you would be surprised at the number of ordinary people out there that think the way I do. They're getting pretty disgusted with the crime problem and how our courts treat them."

"I think we all are, Mike," Vince said. "It's not for us, or them, to act as judge and jury. We just do our jobs, and trust in the system, no matter how fucked up it is."

"Yep. How's the saying go? 'Ours is not to reason why'?"

Vince laughed. "That's the one. But you know, it still bothers me that this psycho is taking the law into his own hands. Nobody has the right to do that."

"People are fed up with these dirt bags getting away with some of the worst crimes," Clark replied. "It seems it gets worse and worse every year. Our justice system is more concerned with the suspects rights than with our citizens' safety."

"Yeah, you're right. But look at us. We're beating our heads against a brick wall getting these guys in custody, only to see them walk free. It's like there's a revolving door on the Hall of Justice."

Vince chuckled. "It sure does seem that way, doesn't it?"

Clark smiled. "Okay, I'll stop my ranting now. All we can do is just do our job the best we can. It isn't our fault these guys are walking."

"Yep," Vince said. "And the way I look at it, there will always be another day. We will get them eventually. It's just too bad that others have to suffer before we do."

"Just something we have to live with, Vince," Clark said. "You ready for another beer? I'm buying."

"I'm ready. One more and I gotta get going," Vince said, signaling the bar maid to bring three more beers.

Chapter 13

It was easy to take him. No one was out in Sachs' neighborhood at that time of the night, and Sachs walked alone to the bus stop to get to work. It was simple to wait in the darkness between the buildings, totally unseen as Sachs walked by, then a quick rush and a strike with the blackjack, knocking him unconscious. It was harder to catch him as he fell and ease him to the ground. Sachs was a big man, bigger than he was, over six feet tall, and somewhat overweight. He left him laying on the sidewalk for the minute it took to get back to the van and drive it up to him, and another two minutes to wrestle the big man into the back.

He closed the side door, then slumped against the van, catching his breath. He looked around, but no one was out on the street to see him. He took out his handkerchief and wiped the sweat off his forehead, then climbed in the passenger door and crawled into the back. Though Sachs was still unconscious, he taped his mouth with duct tape, and used a pair of large nylon flex ties to secure his feet together at the ankles, and another pair to tie his hands behind his back. He rolled the inert body into a large duffle bag, and zipped it up. He drove slowly from the area, softly humming the theme from the old Andy Griffith show.

The next morning, Torelli and Clark were going over Machado's academy file with Lt. Simons.

"No close family in the area," Vince read. "Mother and father both deceased, got an aunt in Eureka." He looked up. "We called her and she said she hasn't seen or heard from him in two years. They're not close. Only other relatives are some cousins and an uncle in Tennessee."

"So he's supposed to be in our area?" Lt. Simons asked.

"That's what the neighbor told us," Clark chimed in. "But we don't know where yet."

Vince said, "Cullin's supposed to be working on a forwarding address through the post office. By the way, where is he?" When Vince had arrived at the office that morning, he had not seen Robbie at his usual spot at the desk.

"He's on his way in. Called to say he had to stop at the post office first. Maybe he'll have some good news for you on that address. How good does this guy Machado look?"

"It's starting to come together, Boss," Vince said. "He's a law and order fanatic, from what we know, has some very strong opinions about crime and punishment, and got kicked out of the academy a few days before the first homicide."

"Only thing," Clark said, "he doesn't fit the description we got from the deputies."

"Is that a real problem, guys, or is it something we can work around?"

Vince took a moment to think. "It's a bit of a problem, but not so much that, by itself, it would eliminate him. Personally, I think this guy looks pretty good, but that's just on the surface. We need more to really convince me he's the one, and to do that, we need to find him."

"So what are you wasting time in my office for? Get out there and find him!"

***

As they were leaving Lt. Simons office, Cullin came in. Pushing his glasses back up on his nose, he said, "Hey, Vince, Mike. Got some good news for you."

"Oh, yeah? And what would that be?" Vince asked.

"Found an address for our boy. Seems he rented a P.O. box a couple of weeks ago for his mail. The box is at one of the Postal Annex stores in the Fil-more. We gonna go stake it out?"

"Did you talk to the owner? See if he has a home address for him?" Clark asked.

"Well, no. I guess I should have, huh?"

"Couldn't hurt," Vince said, smiling at him.

"Okay, then. I'll do that right now."

Muttering to himself, Cullin walked to Clarks' desk, picked up the phone, and began dialing the number he had written on his notepad.

Watching him from the coffee machine across the room, Clark said, "Do we really need him? He sure isn't much help."

"You're right, Mike, he isn't, but the L.T. gave him to us, so we're stuck with him. Besides, he really hasn't gotten in the way or caused any problems. He's just so damn anxious to help. He'll do anything we ask, without question."

"I guess. C'mon, let's get back to work. Hey, Cullin, any luck with that address?"

"Yeah. He changed it to 1440 Sutter Street, Number 307. Wanna go check it out?"

"Sure. Grab your coat," Vince said.

***

Vince drove, with Clark in the front passenger seat and Cullin riding in the back. "How long ago did our boy change his address?" Clark asked, turning to look at Robbie.

"My cousin said they got the change of address two weeks ago. That would make it just before the murders started, right?"

"Yep. That puts him in the City for Barajas' murder."

"Only one thing wrong with that, Mike," Vince said. "How did he know about Barajas? Where would he have gotten the information, and how the hell would he know where Barajas would be and when he would be there? It just doesn't fit."

"Maybe he found out about Barajas from the newspaper, Vince," Mike replied. "It was all over the news, you know."

"Yeah, he probably read it in the Chronicle," Cullin agreed.

"Okay, that's possible, but it still doesn't explain how he was able to get to him. I know," Vince said before either of them could answer. "He could have followed him. But that means he would had to have been here longer than two weeks. It just doesn't make sense to me."

Vince pulled over and parked a block away from the address Cullin had provided. They walked down the street until they got to 1440. Vince swore under his breath when he saw the address Machado listed as his home address was false. It turned out to be a photo shop a few blocks away from the Postal Annex where he had rented the P.O. box.

"God damn it!" Clark swore. "Smart S.O.B., isn't he. Still think he isn't our boy, Vince?"

Vince didn't answer. He just stood there, staring at the storefront, thinking.

"Let's canvas the area, Mike. He must have been here before to get the addresses and rent the P.O. box, so somebody might remember him. Robbie, would you go get his photo from the car? We'll wait here for you to get back."

"Sure, Vince. Be right back."

When Robbie returned with the picture, they walked through the area, covering several blocks, talking to the people walking around and the merchants. They showed Machado's picture to everyone the came across, but no one in the neighborhood could recall seeing him around, including the owner of the postal shop. They returned to the postal annex to see if the owner could recognize Machado. When they asked, the owner said Machado looked familiar, but he couldn't say for sure he was the one who rented the box. "We have 150 boxes, and such a high turnover rate," he said, "I can't remember everyone who rents a box."

Frustrated, Vince asked, "Have you seen him in the area lately?"

"Sorry, Inspector, I can't even say for sure I've ever seen him."

Vince handed him his card, asking him to call if he saw Machado again, then walked with Clark and Cullin to the car.

"A dead end, damn it!" Vince said, pounding the dash of the car with his fist. "This guy is starting to piss me off."

"He's looking better and better, Vince," Cullin said from the back seat. "Giving a false address is not something an innocent person does."

"He's right, you know," Clark said, as he started the engine. "We just might be on to something."

"Shit, Mike, I'm having a hard time believing Machado is our guy. Just doesn't seem right. C'mon, let's go back to the office. We got a ton of paperwork to catch up on. It'll give us time to think on this."

Chapter 14

He walked slowly in the dark toward the abandoned warehouse on the Embarcadero. The sign above the shuttered main door read "Pier 34". He stopped in front and kneeled down, pretending to tie his shoelace. Casually looking around, he saw there was no one else close by. He stood up and tested the large padlock and chain securing the double doors, finding they were intact. He checked the straw he had left wedged between the doors near the bottom and saw it was still in place. He smiled to himself, thinking how easy this has been and how much smarter he was than the cops.

He walked to the side of the warehouse and, with some effort, climbed the chain link gate. Dropping down to the pavement, he crouched in the darkness alongside the building, waiting and listening for a full minute, catching his breath. *Man, I gotta cut that lock off and put my own on there.* Then, sure he had not been seen, he crept along the building until he reached a small side door, also padlocked. He took a key from around his neck, swiftly unlocked the lock and entered the warehouse, softly closing the door behind him. He bolted it from the inside so that he would not be interrupted.

Back in the corner of the warehouse, furthest from the street, sat an old trailer. Several modifications had been made to it to suit his purpose. It had been stripped of everything, leaving only the outer shell, then rebuilt on the inside, with twelve inches of sound deadening insulation attached to the walls, floor, ceiling, and door. Electricity was obtained by tapping into the wires alongside the building. The electricity to the building itself had been shut off several months ago when the City had condemned the building, and forced the tenants to vacate.

He opened the door and smiled at the unfortunate Charlie Sachs, tied naked to the chair in the middle of the trailer.

"It is time, my friend," he said, entering the trailer. "Time to pay the piper."

Charlie's screams could not be heard more than a few feet outside the trailer.

***

Torelli looked around the room, confused at first, then realized it was the jangling of the telephone that had awakened him. As he reached for the phone, he looked at the clock on his nightstand and saw it was 1:45 in the morning.

"Torelli. What's up? When? Okay, freeze the scene. I'll be there within the hour. You call Clark yet? Oh, yeah, call Cullin, the DDA assigned to the case. Dispatch should have his number."

He threw the covers back and sat up in bed, rubbing the cobwebs from his eyes. The phone rang a second time.

"Torelli."

"Vince? It's Liz, Liz Maltby."

"Hey! What's up?" Vince said, as he got out of bed and walked to the kitchen.

"He called me."

"When?"

"Just a few minutes ago. Told me I should go to the intersection of 15th and Berry. He said I better hurry, because the cops were already there and I might miss out on the story."

"Did he say what the story was?"

"Yeah, kinda. He said number three is waiting."

"Shit. Liz, another body's been found. We think it's the third victim."

"I know. I figured it out. Should I go?"

"Yeah, you better. Otherwise he will know something isn't right. Any reporter would jump at the chance to get this scoop."

"I'll be there in 20 minutes. See you at the scene."

"Liz, be careful. He might be watching, so take a look around as you drive there, and be aware of your surroundings once you get to the scene."

"Why, Vince, I'm touched! I thought you didn't like us reporter types!"

"Just be careful, okay? See you there."

"Toodles, Inspector."

***

Vince arrived 40 minutes later. The area had been roped off, and there were several squad cars parked in the street, their emergency lights flashing off the buildings and the usual fog. An ambulance and the Coroner's wagon were parked across the street. A group of officers was standing near a bus stop bench on the corner, sipping coffee from paper cups and talking softly. A yellow plastic shroud covered what appeared to be a body slumped over on the bench. He could see Liz Maltby standing off to the side, talking with one of the officers, making notes on her pad.

"Hey, Torelli, over here," shouted Frank Adamson, the night shift inspector, standing by the body.

Vince walked over to the bench and took the cup of coffee Adamson handed him. "Black, two sugars, right, Vince?"

Taking a sip of the coffee, he said, "That's right. So, fill me in. Who is this guy?"

"This poor, unfortunate person is the late Charlie Sachs, recently paroled from the Solano prison. Charlie worked as a night cook at a neighborhood coffee shop. Charlie killed a family of four, including two small children, while driving home with a snoot full of Wild Turkey. Wanna guess where this happened?" When Vince didn't reply, he said, "I'll take that as a no. Happened right here in this very intersection. How's that for irony. He was convicted of vehicular manslaughter and felony drunk driving. Got paroled after two and an half and moved back to his old neighborhood. Somebody took exception to this."

"Has he been reported as missing yet?"

"Yeah. His boss called last night when he didn't show up for work for the second night. Said he's been trying to reach him for two days without any luck. Charlie wasn't the most likeable person he employs, but he was reliable, if nothing else."

Vince nodded and walked over to the bench. He lifted a corner of the yellow tarp and saw the now familiar cuts on Sach's body. Taking a small flashlight from his pocket, he shined it on Sach's face, carefully examining it. On his left cheek, he could see the number 3 carved into the flesh. He shined the light on his chest, and could see what appeared to be a single stab wound over his heart.

"Damn," he muttered, dropping the tarp over the corpse. He saw Clark and Cullin get out of Clark's car, parked across the street, and walk toward him.

"Hi, Mike, Robbie. It's definitely another one by our boy."

Clark lifted the tarp and looked at the body. "Yep, looks like his handiwork. Who is this?"

Vince told them of Sachs and his background, adding, "There's got to be a message close by, probably on the bench. Mike, check with the Medical Examiner and the forensics team and see when they will be done with the body."

"Okay, Vince. Oh, by the way, that reporter, Liz Maltby, is making a real nuisance of herself. She wants a statement, and asked to talk to you. She said she knows you are the lead investigator."

"All right, Mike. You and Cullin keep an eye on the investigation around the body. Call me if you find anything interesting."

Vince walked over to where Liz was standing with her cameraman. She saw him approaching and had the cameraman begin taping.

"Inspector Torelli, what can you tell us about this homicide? Is this the work of the same suspect, the Retribution Killer?"

"It's too early to tell. We won't know for sure until we get the coroner's report sometime tomorrow."

"C'mon, Inspector, that's a bit of a cop-out. Level with me. It is, isn't it?"

"It appears to be the work of the same suspect, but, like I said, we won't know for sure until tomorrow."

"Any message found around the body?"

"We haven't concluded our investigation, yet. There will be an official statement issued in a few hours. Until it's released, I am unable to provide any more details."

Speaking into the camera, she said, "That was lead investigator, Inspector Vincent Torelli. This is Liz Maltby reporting live from the scene." Liz put her recorder back in her purse and said, "So, you think the killer is watching all this?"

"Yeah, I do. I'd be willing to bet he's close by. He's gonna want to see if you told me about the phone call, so let's keep this short. I'll call you in a couple of hours."

Vince turned and walked away, heading back to the bench and the body. When he arrived, the forensics team was just finishing up. "It's all yours, Torelli. We've done all we can for now. You can move the body if you want. When you're done, let the meat wagon guys know. Have fun."

"Thanks, Andy. By the way, when the coroner gets the body, can you send someone by there to dust it for prints?"

"Sure thing, Vince. See ya."

Vince knelt by the body, carefully examining it again as Clark illuminated it with his flashlight. Finding nothing new, he stood up and then had the officers place the corpse on the ground, on top of the body bag.

As soon as they moved the body off the bench, Vince, Clark, and Cullin saw the white chalk marks, written on the backrest covered by the body. Vince read the words out loud, "The Third Retribution".

"We gotta get this guy, Mike. This is only the beginning. He's not gonna stop until we catch him."

"I know, Vince, I know."

"We'll get him. Don't you worry about that, Vince, we'll get him!" Cullin said, laying his hand on Vince's shoulder.

Vince looked around the scene. He could see nothing in the windows of the buildings, and no suspicious vehicles were parked on the street. There were no bystanders lurking on the corners or in the shadows, but he had that same feeling he had at the high school that the killer was close by, watching them.

Chapter 15

Five hours later, Vince was sitting at his desk, drinking a cup of coffee. Clark was at the coroner's office supervising the printing of the body, and Cullin was back at the DA's office, catching up on his paperwork. Vince took a card out of his pocket, dialed the number, and waited until it was answered.

"Chronicle news room. Liz Maltby speaking."

"Hi, Liz. You busy?"

"Yeah, kind of. Gotta finish the story on this latest killing, Vince. What's up?"

"Can we meet? I got some questions for you."

"Sure. Now is fine with me. Got someplace in mind?"

"See you at Ghiradelli Square, first floor patio, in 30 minutes."

Their call was interrupted by Vince's cell phone ringing. "Hold on, Liz. I've got another call." He fished the cell phone out of his coat pocket and answered it,

"Torelli."

"Vince, it's Mike. We may have gotten lucky. The forensics team found a partial print on Sach's upper arm. I'm on my way back to the office. Want to meet me there?"

"On my way." Speaking into his desk phone to Liz Maltby, he said, "Gotta cancel that meeting, Liz. We just might have that break I was talking about."

"Let me know how it goes, all right? Remember our deal."

"Don't worry, Liz. I won't forget. You keep up your end, I'll keep up mine," he said.

Clark made it back to the Hall of Justice in 10 minutes. As he walked into the homicide office, Vince rushed up to him.

"Got a preliminary match on that print, Vince. It's Machado's!"

"You're sure, Mike? No chance the ID boys made a mistake?"

"Pretty positive match, Vince. Got seven points."

"Guess we better get crackin', then. C'mon, Mike, let's take a ride."

"Where we going, Vince?"

"Back to the area Machado listed as his address. If he knew enough about the area to list a phony address, he's probably living close by. let's see if we get lucky."

***

Vince drove slowly down the street, past the photo shop Machado had listed as his address. He would stop whenever he saw a group of people hanging out and show them Machado's picture, but no one would admit to knowing him. They stopped at the many boarding houses and residential hotels in the area and showed the picture to the managers and any residents they came across, again without finding anyone who had seen him. After an hour of this, Vince parked the car and they walked into each of the businesses in the area, showing Machado's picture to the employees and customers without any luck.

"I'm getting pretty tired of this, Vince," Clark said. "You know somebody we talked to knows this guy. They're just not gonna tell us. This is pissing me off."

"Me, too, Mike. Stay cool, though. These people don't like us and are minimally cooperative now. We start leaning on them and we'll lose them altogether. You getting hungry? How about some lunch?"

"Yeah, Vince. I could use a break. There's a diner just up the block. Wanna try it?"

"Sure. You buying?"

"It's your turn. I got lunch yesterday *and* the bagels and coffee this morning."

"All right," Vince said, with a chuckle. "I'm buying."

They walked in and sat at a booth near the back of the restaurant. The waitress came over and, when she saw who they were, said, "You guys again? I told you an hour ago I don't know that guy."

"Hey, look, we're just here to get something to eat, sweetheart. Can we have a couple of menus, or is that too difficult for you?" Clark said.

She walked off, shaking her head, muttering something about 'dumb-ass cops' loud enough to be heard by the other customers, who started snickering behind their napkins.

"Great, Mike. You've managed to piss her off in less than a minute. That's a record, even for you. I just wonder what surprises we might find in our food, thank you very much."

"C'mon, Vince, she's not going to do anything to our food. It's been a rough day working on a rough case. We're going nowhere fast on this one. We need a break, and soon, or we'll both be climbing the walls."

The waitress returned with their menus, poured them some water, then left without making any more comments. Vince picked up his menu and opened it, causing a small piece of napkin to fall out of it onto the table. Vince could see some writing on it and slowly covered it with his menu. He leaned across the table and whispered to Clark, "Mike, there's a note in my menu."

"What does it say?"

"I don't know, I haven't read it yet."

"Well?"

"Hold on." Vince reached under the menu and pulled the piece of napkin out, laying it flat on the table so no one else could see it. The note was unsigned, and had only an address written on it, with Apartment 2D written below. He slid it across the table to Clark, who read it and said, "Think it's for real, Vince?"

"Don't know, Mike, but it's more than we've gotten until now. It's only a half a block from here. I say we check it out. Follow my lead."

Vince looked around, his voice loud. "Hey, waitress, what's it take to get some service in here? You ignoring us, or just slow?" Turning back to Clark he said, "I think she doesn't like cops, Mike. C'mon, let's get outta this dump. There's another place to eat around the corner." He stood up and walked out, followed by Clark. As he reached the door, he looked at the waitress, who smiled slightly and gave a small "thank you" nod, then turned away.

Vince and Mike left the restaurant and headed toward the address written on the napkin, which Vince had pocketed. When they arrived at the address, he saw it was a two-story residential hotel, the kind that had few amenities, no hot water, and lots of roaches. They had been there showing Machados' picture around less than an hour ago. He looked at the mail slots by the front door and saw the name listed by apartment 2D was "M. Louis."

"M. Louis?" Clark said. "Louis Machado could be M. Louis. How dense am I? I should have realized it sooner."

"Both of us should have, Mike. I looked at the list, too, you know. Don't worry about it. I'll keep an eye on the place, Mike. You go back to the car and call for back-up."

"On my way, Vince. Don't do anything without me." Clark walked away, heading to the car parked a block and a half away. Vince leaned against the building next door, waiting for Clark to return.

From a convenience store across the street, he saw Torelli and Clark approach Machado's building. Anger flared briefly, along with the fear that he had been found out and they were waiting for him to show himself, that they knew Machado had nothing to do with the crimes.

He fished his cell phone from his coat pocket and quickly dialed Machado's number. "C'mon, pick up. Pick up!" he muttered.

"Hello?"

"Louis, get out of there! The cops are coming for you."

"What are you doing calling me here?

"They want you for murder, man. Remember what I told you? They think you're a serial killer. Go out the back way, quickly. They're out front."

"Is this a joke?"

"No joke, man. Look out your window."

"See the guy standing out front? That's Homicide Inspector Vince Torelli. Now, get out of there!"

"But I didn't do anything."

"It doesn't matter. If you even look cross-eyed at them, they're gonna kill you. Go, now." He hung up and looked out the window, watching Torelli as he leaned against the building. *How did they find him?* he thought. *I did everything I could to make him invisible. Changing the name on the mailbox was a particularly brilliant move. It couldn't have been anything I did. He's not that smart, not as smart as me.*

***

Clark jogged up to Vince. "Back-up is on the way. They're sending two beat cars. Should be here in a few minutes."

"Keep an eye out for the back-up units, and watch the front door. I'll be back in a minute."

"Where are you going?"

"Just gonna check out the back, see where the rear door is. I'll be right back."

Vince walked to the end of the building and found a small gate. He reached over it, un-latched the hasp and pushed it open. He walked along the narrow alley between the buildings, being careful of the piles of debris and trash that had accumulated there over the years. He reached the end of the alley and, just as he looked around the corner, he heard feet pounding down the back stairs. Running down the stairs toward him was the one person he had been looking for. He stepped around the corner and shouted, "Machado! Police, hold it right there!"

Machado skidded to a halt, staring at Vince for a few seconds, then turned and ran the opposite way, easily vaulting the low fence separating his building from the shops next door. Vince ran after him, jumping the fence and yelling for him to stop. Machado ran through the adjoining yard and climbed the six-foot chain link fence. Vince followed, hitting the ground running on the other side of the fence. He saw Machado, about thirty feet ahead of him, dodge around a small shed, lower his shoulder, and crash through a rickety wooden fence into the next yard, stumbling as he ran.

Vince followed Machado through the hole in the fence, stumbling on the broken fence boards laying in the tall grass. He regained his balance and ran. Machado dodged around several garbage cans in the yard, and climbed over a low fence into the next yard. Vince followed, dodging the cans and vaulted the fence, seeing Machado run around the corner of the building, now no more that twenty feet away. Vince again shouted for Machado to stop as he ran around the building into the side alley leading to the street. Vince followed, rounding the corner at a full run. As he ran out of the alley onto the street, he crashed into a group of students, knocking three of them down. Tripping over the tangle of arms and legs, he fell to his hands and knees, losing his grip on his gun. As he scrambled to his feet in the middle of the children, who were yelling in terror, he saw his gun on the ground a few feet away. He shoved his way through the tangle of bodies, ran to it and picked it up. When he looked for Machado, he was nowhere to be seen.

"Goddamn it!" he yelled.

Just then he heard running feet coming around the corner of the building behind him. He whirled around, dropped to one knee and aimed at the sound, causing the young students to start screaming again. When he saw it was Clark, he lowered his weapon and slowly stood up.

"You okay, Vince?" Clark asked, lowering his own weapon.

"Yeah. Just pissed off."

"Your hand is bleeding."

Vince looked at this hand and saw it was bleeding from a couple of scrapes on the palm. "Must've happened when I fell."

"Was it Machado?"

"Yeah. He was coming down the back stairs just as I got to the rear yard. I last saw him heading that way," he said, pointing in the direction Machado had run. "Goddamn it! I would've had him if I hadn't tripped over the kids."

"Don't worry about it, Vince. We'll get him soon. Now it's just a matter of time."

"Shit. let's get outta here, Mike."

Just as they got to the front of Machado's building, Cullin drove up.

"Hey, Vince, Mike. I heard your call for backup over the radio. You guys okay? Did you get Machado?"

"We're fine, Robbie," Clark said. "And no, we didn't get him. Almost had him, but he got away." Clark told Cullin what had happened. "Vince scraped his hand up a bit, and his pants are gonna need a repair job, but other than that, he's okay."

"That's good. Anything I can do?"

"Yeah. Get us a search warrant for the apartment."

"You got it. Give me a half hour."

***

An hour later, Vince, Cullin and Clark prowled through Machado's apartment, looking for evidence that would further connect him to the crimes. Nothing was found. Vince pulled Clark off to one side. He looked around, making sure no one else was within earshot.

"Hey, Mike. Don't you think it's strange that we can't find anything here? No evidence, no weapon, nothing?"

"Yeah. There should be something. What about a vehicle? He has to have one. He didn't carry the bodies around with him."

"I've got two of the officers checking all vehicles within a five block radius. I checked out this cup of coffee when we first got in, Mike," Vince said, pointing to the small folding table set up in front of the couch. "It was still warm, and almost full. Two bites gone from the sandwich. He left in an awful hurry."

"Think he made us while we were waiting for the back-up units?"

"Maybe. And maybe someone tipped him off."

"Who would do that?"

"I don't know. A neighbor, maybe. Perhaps the waitress had second thoughts. Maybe the real killer."

"What? The real killer? Still think Machado isn't our killer?"

"In spite of everything we have, Mike, something doesn't fit. The killer knows too much about our investigation, stuff that Machado couldn't possibly know. We keep running into dead ends. Dead-ends provided by the suspect. It just doesn't seem right. I think the real killer wants us to keep wasting our time looking for Machado. That leaves him free to do what he wants. I think that's why he warned him we were coming."

"I'm glad to hear you say that, Vince. I've had the same thoughts lately. What got me thinking was the print we found on Sach's body. How could the killer be so careless? The other dumpsites and the bodies were almost sanitized. He was meticulous in not leaving any clues whatsoever, then all of a sudden he makes a mistake like that? It was too pat, didn't make sense."

"I know. Let's keep this between us for now, okay? Don't tell anyone, even the boss."

"You got it, partner. You know what? If what you think is right, the killer had to have seen us out front of the building, and called Machado to warn him. When we get back, I'm gonna check his phone records, see if he got a call, and if we can locate the caller's number."

"Yeah, sounds good. Let's get back to the office. I'll fill the L.T. in, except our suspicions about the real killer."

"I'm taking you by the hospital first, to get that hand looked at, and don't argue with me, or I'll call Maggie."

"Okay, okay. Let's get it over with. We've got a lot to do."

***

Vince didn't need any stitches. The doctor cleaned the scrapes, then wrapped his hand in a sterile bandage. He gave Vince a tetanus shot, cleared him for full duty, and signed his release form, allowing him to return to work.

When they arrived back at the office, Clark called a contact he had at the phone Company, provided him with the phone number at Machado's apartment, and asked him to run down Machado's record.

"Vince, I called in a favor and he said he would have the info for me in an hour or so."

"Good. let's hope this will provide us with something we don't know," Vince said. Looking around, he leaned in toward Clark and whispered, "We need to go at this a different way, Mike. Right now we're getting nowhere. Whoever is killing these guys, and its not Machado, knows too much about the investigation, and a lot about police procedure, especially evidence. No one can kill three people and leave virtually no clues."

"Yeah, I know. What bothers me is that he always seems to be one step ahead of us, as if he knows what we're going to be doing next. He was there when we found Machado's apartment and called to warn him. Why? Because he didn't want Machado found, 'cause once we eliminated him as a suspect, and we would have in spite of the evidence, we would start looking for him. He wants anonymity. He wants to be free to concentrate on his victims, not worry about how close we are getting."

"I think you're right. You know what, though? We have come close to him, and he didn't like it. Let's re-think how we're gonna go at this. let's go see the boss and talk about it."

"What about Robbie?"

"Where is he?"

"Went back to the DAs office to pick up some stuff. Should be back in a half hour or so."

"Let's get started without him. We'll fill him in when he gets back."

Vince knocked on the door, and entered when the Lieutenant waved them in.

"How goes the battle, Vince?" Lt. Simons asked, leaning back in his chair.

"Not good, Boss." Vince sat down. "You heard what happened when we found Machado's apartment?"

"Yeah. Tough luck." Pointing at Vince's hands he said, "You okay?"

"Fine. Got full clearance from the Doc. Just some scrapes and bruises. Listen, Boss, we think it's time we went at this a different way."

"And what would that be?"

"We need to find out which high profile offenders are being released from custody for whatever reason. Bail, parole, charges dismissed, whatever, but those are our at-risk persons. One of them will be the next victim, and we need to know who it is before it happens."

"Really? C'mon, Torelli. You know how many people in San Francisco fall into that category? What about those in other areas, like Oakland, or Marin County, San Jose, the East Bay?"

"I don't think we need to go that far out. So far our killer has stuck to S.F. cases. I don't think he's gonna change that now. I also don't want anyone else to know what we're doing."

"Why? You think there is a leak somewhere?"

"Maybe." Vince took a deep breath and said, "I've got something I need to tell you. You know Liz Maltby, the Chronicle reporter? She's gotten two calls from our suspect."

"What?" the Lieutenant yelled, causing heads in the investigations office to turn.

"How do you think she got to the scene so quickly the other night? He called her and told her where he had dumped the body."

"So how come I haven't read anything about it in the paper?"

"I've got her convinced to hold off, that it would jeopardize the investigation. I told her she could have first dibs on the story when we break the case if she would cooperate. She agreed. She's gonna call me right away if he calls her back. Maybe, with her help, we'll catch this guy."

"I don't like this, Torelli. You can't trust any reporter, much less that one."

"I know, Boss, but I think we'll be fine with this."

"You know, Torelli, I think the world of you and Clark. You guys are my two best investigators. I'm gonna trust you on this one. By saying not to tell anyone else, does that mean just the three of us know about this?"

"Yes. We'll bring Robbie in on the investigation, but don't tell him about Maltby, or that we think Machado is not our killer."

"All right, Vince. You and Clark get crackin'. And keep me informed of everything from now on."

"Sure, Boss." Vince said, grinning at him.

"Get back to work," Lieutenant Simons said. "Let's get this guy."

***

As Vince and Clark walked back to their desks, Clark's phone rang. "Homicide, Inspector Clark. Yeah, hi. You got it? Good. Yeah. OK. You're kidding? No chance of a mistake? Okay, thanks. I owe ya. See ya."

"That your friend from the phone company?" Vince asked.

"Yep. You're not gonna believe this. The last call Machado got, made at the same time we were out front of his apartment, came from a cell phone. My buddy ran down the number, and, get this, the cell is registered to Machado."

"You're kidding! Damn!"

"Yep. He listed the same postal annex address as his home."

"So that proves someone warned him. Mike, we've got to find Machado and get him to tell us who he gave that phone to."

"Heads up, Vince. Here comes Robbie." Cullin walked over to them and sat next to Vince's desk.

"Hey, guys, what's going on? Any luck with the investigation?"

"Nothing yet. We've got a job for you, Robbie."

"What do you want me to do?"

"Call the local jails, parole offices, prisons, courts, whatever, and find out who's been released to San Francisco in the last couple of weeks. In particular, we're looking for high profile cases like the kind Sachs, Barajas, and Ballinger were involved in. When you come up with a list, try to prioritize the cases by the seriousness of the crime."

"Like what, Vince?" Robbie asked.

"Look at what they did, and list the worst cases first. The kind of case that shows a real cruel angle, or mean streak, or were totally senseless, maybe done just for the thrill of it. Those are the ones I'm looking for. The worse the case, the higher up on the list it should go, okay?"

"Alright Vince, I'm on it! Can I use your desk, Mike?"

"Sure, Robbie. Knock yourself out."

"Thanks."

Cullin grinned at the two of them, turned and quickly walked to Clark's desk, where he sat down and began furiously tapping on the computer keyboard. Vince and Mike looked at each other and smiled, with Vince slightly shaking his head.

Chapter 16

Two days later, Vince, Clark, and Cullin were in Lieutenant Simons' office going over the list of possible victims that Cullin had put together. Cullin handed each of them a file folder.

"So, as you can see, I've listed them by the seriousness of their offense with the most serious first. I've also included their current custody and court status, and, in some cases, the status of pending charges. I've eliminated all those who are in custody and most likely won't be released or be able to make bail. Each name has the current or last known address, and, for those on probation or parole, I've listed their control officer."

"Good work, Robbie," Lt. Simons said, leaning back in his chair. "Vince, Mike, how do you guys want to go at this?"

Vince looked up from the folder. "There are too many here for us to cover all of them. So, Mike, Robbie, and I will go through the list and pick out, oh, let's say, a dozen of the most likely ones and I'll assign someone to watch each of them for the next couple of weeks."

"Sounds good. You're gonna need some more help, so pull four or five guys from the squad here, and get the rest from patrol. I'll make the necessary calls and clear the way for you."

"Thanks, Boss. And thanks to Robbie for the great job he did on this. Good work, Robbie."

Cullin blushed and grinned. "Just doing my job, guys."

"All right, all right. Wanna hold hands and sing Kumbaya?" Lt. Simons growled. "Let's get on this, gentlemen."

They left the Lieutenant's office and gathered around Vince's desk. "Let's prioritize these names. Mike, you and I will cover the top two. I'll pull Jensen, Byers, and White from the squad and assign them the next three. The other seven will be covered by patrol guys. Robbie, keep on top of this. Check every day and see if there are any names we need to add to this list."

"We gonna contact these guys, Vince?" Clark asked.

"Yeah. let's give 'em a call, if we have a phone number. Let them know we think they may be on the killer's list and to keep their eyes open, but don't tell them we will be watching 'em. Looking at this list, I don't think too many of them are gonna give a rat's ass, but at least we did our job and warned 'em."

"Robbie and I will handle that. What're you gonna do?"

"I'm gonna go over this list and compare it against our previous victims to see if there is any connection. Mike, round up Jensen, Byers, and White and ask them to come over here. Robbie, call the patrol desk and ask the watch commander to assign seven of their brightest and best to us, and send them up here."

While Vince waited for Mike to get the other inspectors, he re-read the list Cullin had made, and selected the person he would be watching. When Mike came over with the other three inspectors they went over the list and selected the other four most likely targets. The other seven possible victims were assigned to the patrol officers.

***

At four that afternoon, Vince had gathered the other inspectors and the seven patrol officers around his desk to brief them.

"You patrol officers, sign in on the white board over there. Names, home phone numbers, and cell numbers. I want everyone to list who they are responsible for, and where you will be. Not the whole address, just the street will do. Mike, will you make sure that dispatch has the list of our task force, and the info on the white board?" Turning back to the other inspectors and patrol officers, Vince continued. "If you patrol officers have civvies with you, go change and be ready to leave for your locations by seven p.m. If not, go home and get some. Here's the pictures of the possible victims," he said, spreading them out on his desk. "Pick your guy out and get to know his face. All the info on him is on the back of the photo. You're to stay with him if he goes anywhere, and don't let him know you're following him. Cullin, here, will be notifying them they may be targeted by the killer, but won't be telling them we're watching them. Keep a log of his activities. Stay with him until one in the morning, then you can go home. Be back in my office each day at five p.m. for an update. See your watch commander about flexing your hours and duties, but you're working for me for those eight hours each day. If you need a vehicle, draw one from the motor pool. Lt. Simons has cleared the way, so you shouldn't have any trouble if you tell them you're with the homicide task force. Any questions?"

One of the patrol officers stood up. "Why are we only watching them between seven and one?"

"And you are?" Vince asked.

"Officer James Banks, Sir."

"Because, Officer James Banks, all the victims have been found before 1:30 in the morning. From the nature of the wounds, it's obvious the killer took quite a bit of time killing them. The coroner estimates at least an hour. That means he had to have grabbed them at least two hours earlier, putting the kidnapping within the time frame of seven p.m. to one in the morning." Looking over the group, Vince asked, "Any more questions? Good. Remember, no heroics. If you see anything suspicious, call for backup and wait until they arrive. Now, get going, and be careful."

The task force members took their subjects' photo from Vince's desk and walked out, talking quietly among themselves. Once they had left, Vince turned to Clark, leaned toward him, and said quietly, "Mike, I want you to be careful with this. This killer is close to the investigation and us. He seems to know what we are doing every step of the way, so keep a sharp eye out. If I'm right, he's gonna go after one of the guys you or I are watching. He wants to show us up, to let everyone know how much smarter he is than us. He thinks we can't stop him, and considers this a game."

"Well, he won't get by me. Besides, there's only three others who know we'll be watching these guys."

"Trust me, he'll get that info. Look, all he has to do is follow us. Me one night, you the next. He'll know."

"We'll get him, Vince. This will work. Even if what you say is true. We'll get him."

"I hope so, Mike. I hope so. You all set with your guy?"

"Ray Williams, rapist, currently out on parole after serving a bit more than six years. Victim was a 73-year-old woman. Not enough he had to rape her, he beat her up pretty bad, too. He lives in some flea-bag tenement over in the Bayview district. How about your guy?"

"One Jason Gibbs, 24 years old. He was a youth group leader at St. Andrews Presbyterian Church over in the Richmond District. He's suspected in the molestation of eighteen boys, four to seven years old, including sodomizing a couple of them. Hasn't been charged yet, as the investigators and D.A. are having a hard time pinning the victims down to specific dates they were abused."

"Man, a couple of real losers."

"You know it, but prime candidates for our suspect."

"Yeah. You know, it wouldn't be much of a loss if he got to them."

Vince laughed softly. "You got that right. Ah, well, as they say, 'ours is not to reason why'."

Clark smiled at Vince. "You want to get some dinner? We got a couple of hours yet."

"Yeah. Let me call Maggie and I'll be right with you. Get the car and I'll meet you downstairs."

"On my way."

Vince called home and told Maggie he would be late. He told her briefly what he would be doing, said he loved her, and hung up after her usual "Be careful, Hon," warning. He then called Liz Maltby and told her about the stakeouts. He asked her to call him on his cell phone immediately if she heard from the suspect, and assured her he would let her know if anything broke on the case. He hung up and met Clark downstairs.

Chapter 17

Four days later, Vince, Clark, and Cullin were in the office with the other inspectors and patrol officers. None of them had seen anything unusual since they had begun the surveillance detail.

Watching the possible victims was a difficult job, as they moved around frequently, visiting the seedier places in the city. Pool halls, porn theaters, bathhouses, bars, and bookie joints all enjoyed their company. The inspectors and officers had a difficult time keeping from being made, but so far had avoided any unwanted attention. Their charges were none the wiser that they were being followed.

After the briefing that afternoon, they left the office to begin the evening's surveillance. Vince, Clark, and Cullin sat around Vince's desk for a few more minutes, finishing their coffee, before Cullin said goodnight and left for the day. Vince and Clark left to begin what they jokingly called the "babysitters detail".

Vince drove to the Richmond District rooming house where his subject, Jason Gibbs, lived. Vince quickly found out that Gibbs mostly stayed in his apartment in the evenings. He had left his room only three times in the four days Vince had been watching him, and then only to walk a couple of blocks to a local diner, or to the neighborhood video store. He was always back by nine p.m., and turned his lights out by eleven when he went to bed. Vince had to fight the boredom of sitting in his car each night while Gibbs slept peacefully in his bed.

He turned on the radio, tuning it to a soft rock station, and turned the volume just loud enough to hear. It was cold in the city. The fog was rolling in, coloring the city gray, and a steady wind was blowing. A slight drizzle from the heavy fog covered the windshield, making visibility difficult. He didn't dare turn on his wipers, and with the engine off, the cold seeped into the car.

He watched Torelli sitting in the car from a darkened alley across the street, watched him wipe off the condensation from inside the windshield. He had parked on the street behind Gibbs' apartment and walked through the connecting alley, stopping a few feet back from the entrance to Gibbs' street in the deeper shadows, where the street lights couldn't reach. He was safe there, in the darkness, and being so close to his adversary, the great Inspector Torelli, thrilled him. He could just walk up to the car, pull the Smith and Wesson from his waistband, and BANG BANG! Two to the head, no more Inspector Torelli.

The thought of shooting him sent a shiver down his spine. *No!* he thought. *Not tonight. There is so much more to the game. It is not his time to die, not just yet.* He thought how much fun it would be when he kidnapped Gibbs right under the great inspector's nose, and how he would leave his body at the church. He could imagine how pissed off Torelli would be, and that made him smile. He softly began to hum an old

Beatles tune as he continued to watch him from the alley.

***

At 8:45, Gibbs walked out the door of his apartment building and turned left toward the video store three short blocks down the street. Vince let him get a half a block away before he got out of the car and followed him, walking on the opposite side of the street. The fog had thickened to where it was difficult to see more than a shadow from across the street and, along with the darkness, Vince had no fear of being spotted. He stopped across from the video store as Gibbs entered and headed toward the back, looking at the many videos and DVDs lined along the walls. Vince knew Gibbs would be in the store for no more than ten minutes, as usual, before heading back to his apartment. He caught a glimpse of him now and then in the store's bright lights through the front window as he wandered around. He yawned, fighting the boredom, and turned up the collar of his overcoat, trying to keep the dampness off his neck.

Vince casually watched the other customers entering and leaving the store, not paying much attention to them, waiting for Gibbs to come out. He glanced at his watch and saw it had been a little over ten minutes since Gibbs had entered the store. He looked through the front window, trying to find him, but he was nowhere in sight. Vince did not become alarmed yet. After all, Gibbs had only been in there a couple of minutes longer than usual. He leaned back against the building and waited, confident Gibbs would be coming out any time now.

He waited five more minutes before he crossed the street and looked through the front window. He could see most of the store from there and scanned the video racks looking for him. He became uneasy when he couldn't see Gibbs, but decided to wait another couple of minutes in case Gibbs was behind one of the racks, out of sight. Two more minutes passed without Vince seeing Gibbs, two minutes in which his uneasiness grew, almost becoming panic. He decided he couldn't wait any longer and went inside. His anxiety grew as he walked through the store, looking for Gibbs and not seeing him. He checked the entire store, including the restroom without finding him. He went to the checkout counter and flashed his badge. Showing him the picture of Gibbs, he asked, "Seen this guy in here tonight?"

"Yeah. That's Jason. Why do you want to know?"

"I need to talk to him. He may be a witness to something that happened near here. Is he still here?"

"I don't know. Last I saw him, he was over there," the clerk said, pointing toward the back of the store.

"Is there a back door to this place?" Vince asked. The clerk pointed to the back room, and Vince ran through the store and out the door, which led to a dimly lit alley.

As he burst out the door, he heard an engine revving and tires screeching at the end of the alley. Looking to his right, he saw a light colored van accelerating around the corner. He ran to the end of the alley, certain that Gibbs was in the van, but by the time he got to the street, the van was nowhere to be seen. Vince cursed to himself, pulled his two-way radio from his jacket pocket and put the call out. He gave the van's description, it's last direction of travel, and Gibbs' description, hoping there was a patrol unit in the area, knowing it would do no good even if there was. He then called dispatch on his cell phone asking for a crime scene unit and the sector units to respond. He walked back to the door and slammed it with both hands as hard as he could several times, yelling at the top of his lungs. When the beat officers arrived, he was sitting calmly on a box next to the door.

***

The killer drove at the speed limit across the city, parking in the darkened lot by his "workshop", as he liked to think of it. He crawled into the back of the van and rolled Gibbs into a large steamer trunk, then opened the back doors, took a hand truck out, and slid the trunk onto it. The few people walking by on the Embarcadero paid him no attention. Dressed in dark cover-alls, he looked like one of the workmen common to the area. He opened a small gate in the chain link fence on the side of the building, and wheeled the trunk along the side, keeping to the shadows, to the side door. He unlocked the door and wheeled the unfortunate Jason Gibbs inside. He carefully closed the door, latching it from the inside, then wheeled the trunk to the trailer and opened the door.

***

Vince and Clark finished interviewing all the employees and customers in the store. No one remembered seeing Gibbs leave, though they did remember him wandering around the store. The crime scene crew was processing the back door for prints, and photos had been taken of the tire tread marks found where the van had been parked. Several sets of prints were found on the door, all eventually identified as belonging to employees. Once again they came up empty.

It was close to one a.m. when he got back to his office. Vince paced the floor, venting to the other members of the surveillance team. "Goddamn it! The son of a bitch took him right under my nose. That prick knew I was watching him, and did it anyway, just to prove a point. He's out there now, laughin' his ass off, feeling superior."

"Easy, Vince. Maybe it was just a coincidence," Clark said, trying to mollify him. No one else in the room dared say anything, given Vince's mood.

"No coincidence, Mike. He knew I was there. That's why he waited until Gibbs went to the video store. That's why he took him in a public place. He's on top of the game, Mike. He likes outsmarting us. Goddamn it!" Vince flung himself into his desk chair. "Did you get hold of Robbie?"

"Not yet. I'll keep calling. I think he's at a cousin's place in Red Bluff."

"No rush, now. I got a feeling we're gonna be here most of the night. We got lots to do." Turning back to the rest of the task force, Vince assigned them their duties. Most he sent back out to the streets to look for the van he saw leaving the back of the store. He had them concentrate along the wharf areas, both north and south of Market Street.

Chapter 18

The killer pulled the knife from Gibbs' chest, watching his life ebb. He listened as Gibbs drew his last breath, heard the death rattle, saw the light go out of his eyes. He shuddered, feeling an almost sexual release from the murder. He smiled as his eyes filled with tears, blurring his vision. He stroked Gibbs' face, peering deeply into his dead eyes. A tear trickled down his cheek as he carefully carved a "4" on Gibbs' face.

He stepped from the trailer and stood on a plastic sheet on the warehouse floor. He unzipped the cover-alls, placing them in the green garbage sack. He was naked underneath. He removed his latex gloves and the shower cap, placing them in the bag, too. Sitting on the floor, he removed the surgical shoe covers from his feet and added them to the bag. He then stepped off the plastic, rolled it up and placed it in the bag with the clothing. He added two large chunks of broken concrete, tied the bag shut, wrapped duct tape around the knot, and placed the bag aside. Later, he would throw the bag off the end of the pier outside his workshop, to join the other bags he had tossed there.

He put on a new pair of latex gloves, then grabbed a clean pair of cover-alls and pulled them on, zipping them all the way up. He put on an old pair of shoes he bought earlier at a thrift store, and donned a dark baseball cap purchased with the shoes, then went back in the modified trailer. He checked Gibbs' carotid pulse; finding none, he removed the nylon flex cuffs binding him to the chair, pulled him out and onto the cheap shower curtain he had purchased earlier that day. Rolling Gibbs' body up in the curtain, he slid it into an over-sized plastic bag and closed the top. With some difficulty, he placed the body in a large, cheap trunk he had purchased, then got the hand truck to wheel it out to the van he had stolen early that morning.

The van was parked three blocks up and across the street. If the police checked it, they would find no reason to suspect it was involved. He had stolen a dark blue van, once again from the long term parking at Oakland Airport. The van would be abandoned within the next hour, again in Oakland, near the docks, and the clothing discarded in a dumpster a few miles away. His car was parked a few blocks from the Port of Oakland with a change of clothes in the trunk. He made a mental note to make this the last time he got his vehicles from the airport. He knew it would not be long before Torelli put two and two together and figured it out. He was a worthy adversary; worthy, but not equal. He smiled again, pleased with himself, and began whistling the theme to Leave It to Beaver.

***

Liz Maltby was jarred awake by the jangling of her phone. She opened one eye and looked at the clock next to her bed, seeing it was just after two in the morning. She groaned, and reached for the receiver.

"Liz Maltby. I hope for your sake this is important."

"Ah, Miss Maltby. Sorry to wake my favorite reporter, but you may be interested to know there has been another retribution."

She sat up in bed, instantly awake. "Is this who I think it is?"

"Very possibly, my dear. In about five minutes, I will be calling the police to report a body on the steps of Saint Andrews Presbyterian Church. If you hurry, you may get there before Inspector Torelli."

"Wait! Don't hang up. Can you tell me who it is?"

"Certainly," he replied, his voice muffled by the cloth he had placed over the mouthpiece of the phone. "Ready to write this down?"

"Hold on just a second," she said. Liz turned on the lamp next to the bed, then pulled open the drawer of the nightstand and grabbed a pencil and small tablet she kept there. "Okay, go ahead."

"Jason Gibbs, Miss Maltby, a felon most foul. Mr. Gibbs liked to molest little boys while he posed as a youth ministry teacher at Saint Andrews Church in the Richmond District."

"Why are you doing this? Why not let the courts handle it?"

"That's just the point, Miss Maltby. The courts aren't handling it. They let scum like Gibbs go for the most ridiculous reasons. People like him, and the others, need to pay for their crimes, Miss Maltby."

"And if the courts don't do it, what gives you the right to do it?"

There was only silence on the line.

"Are you there?" she asked.

"Miss Maltby," he said softly, "I am trying to enlighten you, yet you choose to question my motives. It should be clear to a woman of your intelligence. Do not question me again, Miss Maltby. This conversation is over."

There was a soft click on the line. "Wait, I'm sor..." She knew it was too late, that he had hung up. "Damn!" she muttered, as she quickly got out of bed and threw on some clothes. As she drove to the church, she took out her cell phone and dialed Vince's number.

***

He had placed Gibbs' nude body on the front steps of the church, propping him upright as if he was sitting there waiting for it to open. He parked the van two blocks down and around the corner, then walked back to the apartment building across the street from the church, talking to Liz Maltby as he walked. After he hung up, he pulled a Buck knife from his pocket, jimmied the front door, entered the small lobby, and went up the stairs to number 3C. He used the knife again to pry open the door of the vacant apartment, forcing the ancient lock with almost no noise and little damage. He pulled the cheap plastic lawn chair he had brought there yesterday to the window and sat down. Looking out over the front of the church, he took out his cell phone and dialed 911, waiting for the operator to answer.

Chapter 19

Vince and Clark arrived to find Liz Maltby already there. She had called Vince and told him of her call from the killer. The usual fog had rolled in, and a fine mist was in the air, coating everything and everyone, chilling the air. Vince could see wisps of fog rolling past the streetlights as he and Clark walked toward the crime scene. He pulled his coat a bit tighter around his neck, trying to keep the damp out.

From his chair by the window, in the dark, he watched Torelli, Clark, and the other officers fussing about the crime scene, but mostly he was watching Liz Maltby. He saw her when she arrived 15 minutes after the first officers, watched as she directed her photographer which angles to shoot from, watched as she interviewed the patrol officers who found the body, and watched as she greeted Torelli and Clark when they arrived. Something about the way she looked around while talking to Torelli caught his attention. It was as if she was checking to see if there was anyone nearby that may overhear them.

Why would she do that? he thought. *Why is she so worried someone may hear her? Is she conspiring with him against me? Are they planning something?* He took a small pair of binoculars out of his pocket and studied her face as she spoke. He could see she was not writing anything down and the photographer was nowhere around. This was no interview. He pulled his phone from his pocket and dialed her cell number.

Her cell phone ringing interrupted their conversation. She excused herself and walked a few feet away before answering. "Liz Maltby."

He spoke to her as he watched her through the binoculars. "Miss Maltby. Getting everything you need for your story?"

She started frantically waving at Torelli, trying to get his attention. When he looked at her, she pointed to the phone and mouthed, "Its him."

"Yes, I am. You will see the story in tomorrow's paper. Anything I should know?"

"Are you going to include our conversation earlier?"

"How can I?" she asked. "That would mean I would have to tell someone about our calls."

"I think it's too late to worry about that, don't you?"

"What do you mean?" she asked.

"How long has Torelli known about my calls?"

"I don't know what you are talking a bout."

"Now, don't lie to me. I saw you talking with him tonight. That was no interview. What were you talking about, Miss Maltby? Perhaps a way to catch me? Devising a trap, were you?"

"No, no. You don't understand. We were just chatting. Talking about small things, nothing in particular."

"Don't lie to me!" he shouted into the phone. "I am not stupid, Miss Maltby. Please don't treat me as such."

"I'm sorry. I meant no insult."

After a short pause to get himself under control, he said, "I will consider accepting your apology. Now, from here on out, you will *not* tell Inspector Torelli, or any other member of the investigative team, anything we talk about, unless I tell you to. That includes this conversation."

"And if I do?"

"That, Miss Maltby, you will regret. Until now, I have concentrated on criminals. That can change, should I feel I have been betrayed. Do you understand what I am saying, Miss Maltby?"

Liz shivered at his words, and softly replied, "Yes, I understand," she said, fear washing over her.

"Write your story, Miss Maltby. Write it well. I will decide after I read it whether I will call you again, or pay you a visit. Now, make it so."

He hung up the phone.

Liz slowly brought the phone down from her ear, placing it in her pocket.

"Liz?" Torelli asked, "What's going on?"

Not looking at Vince she whispered just loud enough for him to hear, "I can't tell you now. That call was from the killer. I'll call you in the morning." She then walked over to the news van and got in, telling her photographer to drive away.

"What was that all about, Vince?" Clark asked.

"I don't know, Mike. She got a call from the killer. Something's going on, but she didn't tell me what. She said she'll call me in the morning." They saw the Medical Examiner had arrived, so Vince said, "There's the M.E. We'll talk about this more later."

***

Vince was at his desk by 8:30 a.m., sipping on a steaming mug of coffee, reviewing the case file. Clark came in a couple of minutes later, yawning, holding his own cup of coffee.

"Hey, Mike. Come here. I want you to look at this."

"What's up, Vince?"

"Look at this set of prints. This is Machado's print card, the one from which the print on Barajas' body was identified. It was the right index finger, wasn't it?"

"That's right. Why?"

"Well, there is a label over that print space, the kind we use if the print is screwed up. We stick the blank white label over the messed up print and re-roll a good print on it."

"Yeah, so?"

"You know I don't think Machado is our guy, so what if the prints have been altered? What if some-one took a print card, changed the info so it ap-peared to be Machado's, then placed Machado's right index print over the real right index print?"

"That's pretty far fetched, Vince."

"Yeah, maybe so, but maybe we should check it out?"

"By we, you mean me. Okay, I'm on it. I'll hand carry this card to the I.D. bureau and see what they have to say."

"Thanks, Mike."

"I'm going home after I take these prints over there. I'll tell the print guy we need the results first thing in the morning."

"Sounds good. I'll see you this afternoon, then, at the briefing?"

"I'll be there. You should go home, too. Get a few hours sleep. We've been here all night, Vince."

"Can't just yet. I've got a couple of things to do. I'll probably not go out with you guys tonight."

"All right. See you later."

A few minutes later Vince's phone rang. "Homicide, Torelli."

"Vince. It's Liz. Can you talk?"

"Hold on a minute." Placing his hand over the mouthpiece, he looked around to see if anyone was in earshot. None of the other inspectors were in the room, and Cullin was standing at the coffee machine talking with one of the secretaries. "Go ahead, Liz."

"He called me again, Vince. He called when we were at the crime scene last night. He was watching us."

"He was? How do you know?"

"He said things that he could only know if he was there watching. He got angry when we were talking. He guessed we were sharing information, and told me to play it straight with him, not to lie to him. He threatened to 'pay me a visit' if I continued to talk with you, lied to him, or if he thought we were trying to trap him."

"Shit, Liz. You all right?"

"Yeah, just scared. Vince, I don't know if I will call you again. If he calls me, I mean. I just don't know."

"It's okay, Liz. You do what you think is right. I don't want you take any chances."

"Thanks, Vince. Take care."

"Before you go, will you tell me what he said? His exact words?"

She related what the killer said, including that he told her to write her story. "He said 'write it well', and that he would read it before deciding whether he would call me again, or pay me a visit."

Vince heard the catch in her voice. "Liz, it's all right. I'm sorry to put you through this, but it's important. Was that it? Did he say anything else?"

"No. Wait, yes there was. After he told me to write the story, he said 'Make it happen'. No, that wasn't it. Oh, yeah, he said 'Make it so'. That was it, 'Make it so.'"

"Thanks, Liz. You be careful. Don't go anywhere alone after dark, just in case. And pay attention to your surroundings when you're driving around, or going home."

"All right, I'll be careful. Bye, Vince."

"Bye, Liz."

Vince slowly hung up the phone, and turned back to the case file. He couldn't concentrate on the reports, though, his thoughts racing at what Liz had told him. *The son of a bitch was there, watching us. He was there. He took Gibbs from under my nose, then hung around to watch, the prick.* Vince slammed his fist down on the desk, causing Cullin and the secretary to look in his direction.

"It won't happen again, God dammit," he muttered out loud.

"Vince? You alright?" Cullin had come over to his desk. "What won't happen again?"

"Nothing, Robbie. Never mind." Vince took a deep breath, then asked, "You find any more possible victims?"

"None that seem to fit our profile. There are a couple possibles, but their crimes don't fit. One is a crank dealer and small time enforcer. His only victims are other dirt bags. The other is a con man who scammed the life savings from an elderly couple. The old man died of heart failure because he lost his life savings. I don't think either one falls into the killer's area of interest."

"Thanks, Robbie. Good work."

"You gonna go back out tonight? Got a new possible to watch?"

"Not tonight. I'm going home, spend some time with the family."

"There ya go. Get some rest. Things will be better in the morning."

"I doubt that. Listen, you take care. Apparently that psycho is watching us, so we all may be in danger."

"Really? Wow! I will be careful, then."

Vince got up from the desk and grabbed his coat. "I'm going home. See you in the morning."

During the drive home, he couldn't get the phrase the killer said out of his mind. *Make it so,* he thought. *Same phrase he used when he took Mitch Ballinger from the van on its way to Atascadero. Where have I heard that before?* Try as he would, he could not remember. It was right there, on the edge of his memory, swirling, yet refusing to be recognized. He shook his head, clearing his thoughts, and concentrated on his driving. He dialed his home on his cell phone, and when she answered, told Maggie he was on his way and would be there soon.

Chapter 20

The next morning, the killer got up early, anxious to read the paper. He went outside in his robe and slippers and picked up the paper from the front porch. Standing there, he opened it up and flipped through the front section until he found the article on his latest project. He was disappointed that it was on page six instead of the front page, where it belonged. He read the headline and smiled to himself. "Retribution Killer Leaves Fourth Victim At Church."

He went inside and sat at the kitchen table with his coffee and read the rest of the article. The radio behind him, playing softly, was tuned to the oldies station. When he finished the article, he picked up the phone and dialed the Chronicle's phone number.

***

Liz arrived at the paper at 9:30, grabbed her mail and messages from her mailbox and walked to her office. She stopped in the break room and got a cup of coffee. When she got to her office, she tossed the mail into her in basket, sat down, took a sip of coffee and started looking through her messages.

She almost dropped her cup when she saw the message from "The RK." Her hand trembled as she read, "The article was fine. I approve. I have postponed our visit. I will call you later." Liz grabbed the phone and started to dial Vince's desk. Half way through, she stopped and softly replaced the handset back on the cradle. She crumpled up the message sheet and dropped it in her wastebasket.

***

Vince walked into the office to his phone ringing. Clark was already there, walking towards him with two cups of coffee. Vince walked quickly to his desk and picked up the phone as Clark handed him his coffee.

"Torelli."

"Good morning, Vince. Jacobs, here."

Steve Jacobs had worked in the forensics services division of the police department for the last eighteen years, and was the unofficial expert in the fingerprint identification bureau. He had a solid reputation with the District Attorney's office, and many defense attorneys, as a professional in his field of expertise. They knew that if he was called as an expert witness in fingerprint comparison that his testimony would be solid and unimpeachable. Many times the comparisons he made provided the critical link that convicted the defendant. He was the person to whom Clark had taken Machado's print card.

"Tell me something I don't know, Steve. I need help, here."

"Information is what I have, Vince, but I don't think it's what you expect to hear."

"Aw. Shit. Don't tell me you couldn't identify the prints. Those aren't Machado's prints."

"Actually, they are."

"What? I know the right index is his, cause that's what matched the print on the body, but who do the rest of the prints belong to?"

"That's what I'm saying. All the prints are Machado's, except the right index."

"You're shittin' me, Steve. Don't fuck with me over this, I'm not in the mood."

"I'm not, Vince. The print card is Machado's. I've compared it with another of his cards and they match. I got the correction label off the card and the print underneath is Machado's. The only print I can't I.D. is the one that was placed over Machado's print."

"You run it through the state print identification system, and the FBI? Did you check our in-house system?"

"Yes, yes, and yes. No luck. Whoever owns that print hasn't been arrested in California, and has no record with the FBI."

"Damn. Listen, keep checking, that unidentified print belongs to our killer."

"Will do, Vince. I'll let you know if I come up with anything. 'Bye."

"Thanks. Talk to you soon."

Clark had perched on a corner of Vince's desk during the phone call and asked, "No luck on the prints?"

"Nope. Whoever this guy is, he's smarter than I thought. I think we've under-estimated him. He somehow got hold of Machado's prints, placed a correction label over the right index finger, and rolled another print on it."

"Arrogant little bastard, isn't he?" Clark said, sipping his coffee.

"That he is. I'd be willing to bet that print belongs to our killer. He's got to know his prints aren't on file. Why else would he take such a chance?"

"He likes the game, Vince. He's proving to himself again and again how much smarter he is than we are. At least, he thinks he is. He gets a kick out of this."

"His ego will be his downfall, Mike. I just hope it happens before he kills again. What really bothers me is that this guy must be a lot closer to us than we think. If he has access to the print files, then he has been on top of the investigation from the beginning."

"Yeah, I know what you mean. Is Jacobs doing a search of our in-house print files? How about the FBI and the automated print identification system?"

"Already have him doing it. Just gotta wait to see if he gets a hit."

"I guess that's all we can do," Clark said, sighing. "What's on tap for tonight, Vince? You going out to baby-sit someone?"

"Don't know, Mike. I've got a play at Scott's school I promised I'd go to. We're supposed to go to pizza first, then to the play."

Cullin walked over and sat in the chair next to Vince's desk. "You gotta go, Vince. You promised him. Besides, the time off will do you good."

"Yeah, I know." He looked from Clark to Cullin, then back again. "You guys convinced me. I'm going to the play."

"Good," Clark said. "Now, I'll be out tonight and I'll call you if anything happens. I don't think he'll hit again this soon. It's only been two days, and he usually waits a week or so before going after his next victim."

"Yeah, Vince," Cullin said. "It will be a quiet night. Don't worry about it. Go have a good time with your family."

Later that afternoon, Vince attended the briefing for the surveillance squad, admonishing them to be extra careful. He told them he would be on call, and if anything unusual happened, to radio for help immediately, then call him on his cell phone.

After the rest of the team left, Vince was alone in the office. He called Steve Jacobs and asked him to do some special research and comparisons.

"If you get anything, call me on my cell phone, Steve, not the office phone, and call *only* me. Anytime, day or night."

"Okay, Vince, though I think this is a waste of time. But, I only work here, so I'll give it a try and let you know as soon as I find out anything."

"Thanks, Steve. Keep this between us. I don't want anyone else to know what we're doing."

"All right. Call you later."

Chapter 21

Vince was just leaving the restaurant with his family, on their way to the play, when his cell phone rang. He looked at his wife and said, "Sorry babe, but I gotta get this." Maggie smiled, shook her head, and walked toward the car with the boys.

"Torelli," Vince answered.

"Vince, this is Robbie. Sorry to bother you, but I thought I better call you."

"What's up, Robbie?"

"Sausalito police recovered a body from the bay, shot twice in the head by a large caliber pistol."

"This another one by our guy?"

"Probably. We think it's Machado."

"Aw, shit. Are they certain it's him?"

"Pretty sure. Still had his wallet on him with his ID. The body is at the Marin County morgue. They're checking prints now, but it's just a formality."

"They say how long he was in the water?"

"According to the M.E., not more than 24 hours, probably a bit less."

"So that means he was killed last night or early this morning. You said he was shot?"

"Yeah. Sausalito cops say it was a large caliber pistol, probably either a .45 or .40 caliber semi auto. Both the wounds were through and through, so there won't be any bullets recovered."

"Did you call Clark?"

"Yeah. He's on his way over there. So am I. You want to meet us?"

"Not if Mike is on his way. Not much I could do that he can't. Keep me posted, though. I'll bet our suspect left something on or near the body. He wants us to know it was him. Have Mike stay close to the body, okay? I want him, and you, to keep an eye on the evidence collection. Inventory everything yourself. Take some photos, too, if you have a camera."

"Okay, Vince. I'll let Mike know and we'll get back to you."

"I'm gonna be at the play with the family, so my phone will be off, but I will leave my pager on. Call and leave me a message if you find anything."

"Got it, Vince. Talk to you later."

Vince disconnected the call and as he placed the phone in his pocket, it rang again.

"Damn! What now?" he muttered as he answered the call, "Torelli."

"Vince, it's Liz."

"Hey, Liz. How ya doing?" Vince was surprised by her call. It had been several days since he last talked to her, when she had said she wouldn't be calling him anymore.

"Okay, Vince. Look, let's cut the small talk. It took a lot for me to call you, so let me talk before I lose my courage."

"Sure, Liz. You get another call from our friend?"

"Yeah, about 20 minutes ago. He told me a body had been found. He wants me to write a story about how baffled the police are, that they are unable to make any progress on the case. He wants me to emphasize how the killer has always been one step ahead of the authorities. Vince, I don't know what to do. I can't write a story like that. And what's more, my editor is not going to print something like that, but if I don't write it, the killer may come after me."

"Did he threaten you again?"

"Yeah, kind of. He said he would read the story before deciding whether he could trust me. He said he wanted it on the front page. Said he hoped he wouldn't have to pay me a visit."

"Did he say anything else?"

"Yeah. Not to call you."

"Did he mention me by name, or just mean don't call the police?"

"He knows your name. He said, 'Don't call Torelli'. And when he was done, he said that phrase again. You know, 'Make it so, Ms. Maltby, make it so'."

"Look, Liz, I know what it must have taken for you to make this call. Can you talk to your editor about this? See if he will go along and print the story. If he agrees, go ahead and write it, but don't put it on the front page. Page three or four would be okay. Then, take a vacation for a couple of weeks. Get out of the city. Go to Tahoe, or L.A., or Disneyland. Just get away for a while. I'm gonna put a trace on your phone. We'll monitor it and see if we can't get him that way."

"All right, Vince, but I'm not leaving town. I'll check into a hotel or something."

"It would be better if you left the area, you know."

"Yeah, I know it would, but I've thought about this for a while, and I'm ashamed I let that psycho make me do things I don't want to. I'm going to stick around."

"Well, if that's what you want. Be careful, though. Take roundabout routes home and to work, and watch for suspicious cars following you. This guy is smart, and he's dangerous."

"I know, Vince. I'll talk to my editor. And Vince?"

"Yeah, Liz?"

"Thanks. I'll be in touch."

"Just be careful."

***

A few minutes after the call to Vince, her cell phone rang. She answered the call, listened for a minute, then said, "It's done. I just got off the phone with him. He thinks I'm terrified, but that I'm sticking around to do my civic duty to help catch you. By the way, he's going to tap my phone here at work, so be careful when you call. Yeah, I will. Look, don't threaten me! Remember we have a deal, and I can make it pretty hot for you, too. The information I got today is stashed away, and the cops would be real interested in it. No, I won't tell you who gave it to me, but it was enough that I have a good idea who you are, so if anything happens to me, it goes to the cops. I only agreed to do this so I would get exclusive information. All right, all right. Call me when you have something." She hung up the phone, muttering, "Psycho asshole."

He hung up the cell phone and thought, *I'll have to do something about her. She's becoming a liability and dan-*

gerous. He dialed another number, and when his call was answered, told the person about his conversation with her.

Chapter 22

San Francisco Chronicle
Editorial
Police Protection Fairly Applied?

The Retribution Killer claimed his fourth victim last night, leaving the mutilated body on the steps of Saint Andrews Church in the Richmond District, and we are wondering whether the police are really trying their best to catch the killer, as they claim.

Granted, the killer's victims are not what we would call pillars of society, but they are citizens of this city and regardless of their background, they deserve the same protection as others.

Is it possible that because of the victim's status, their murders are not receiving the same attention as our law abiding citizens? Is the "Retribution Killer Task Force" merely for show? How serious is the Police Department in pursuing all possible leads to identify the killer?

Police officials have denied there is anything less than a full effort in the investigation of this case, and point to the fact that the task force consists of five full time investigators, a deputy district attorney, and seven officers. Lead investigator, Inspector Vincent Torelli, declined comment when we called his office, referring us to his commanding officer, Lieutenant Simons.

Lieutenant Simons told us this case has the highest priority and they are following all leads fully. He also said they have a "person of interest" they wished to talk to that they were trying to locate at this time. He stopped short of calling this person a suspect. He refused to identify this person, claiming it would jeopardize the investigation.

Whatever the police are doing, they need to do it better. We cannot allow vigilante killers loose on our streets, nor can we allow our police department, our public safety officers, to do less than their best to bring this killer to justice, regardless of whom the victims are.

We call upon Chief Phillips to investigate the Department's performance, and provide full disclosure of his investigation. No, rather we demand it, as do the citizens of San Francisco.

Vince was at his desk by six a.m., going over the reports from the Sausalito police Department. In particular, he was interested in the evidence list. He already knew what was there, as Cullin had called him late last night when the business card was found.

During the inventory of the contents of Machado's pockets, the Sausalito police had found one of Vince's water-soaked business cards. Written on the back was *What now, Torelli?* It was signed, *The RK.* Vince would have the forensics team try to analyze the handwriting, and fume the card for fingerprints, but he knew this would be fruitless. The killer had written the message with a pen, but the water had blurred the writing to where it was useless for a comparison, and no prints would be found. Still, he had to at least try.

Vince looked carefully through the list for something, anything, that would lead to the killer's identity. The police ID tech had air dried Machados' clothes and shoes, then scraped them over a clean sheet of white paper, turned out and vacuumed the pockets, and collected whatever was on the paper. She had found grayish fibers on Machado's shoes and pant legs that appeared to come from a carpet, but nothing else that survived the submersion in the bay. Vince planned to call her later that morning and ask her to notify him when she had any information on the fibers.

Later that day, Steve Jacobs called Vince to his office.

"Okay, Steve, what have you got?" Vince asked.

"I checked the prints you asked me to against that print from Sach's body with negative results. It doesn't belong to any of them."

"God damn it. I was so sure."

"Well, it's gotta be a relief to know the suspect isn't one of your co-workers."

"Yeah, that's true. But, it still doesn't make sense to me. The only way the suspect could stay one step ahead of us is if he knows what we know, and the only people who have that information are in the office. You're sure, Steve? There's no chance of a mistake?"

"No chance, Vince. I double-checked each print from everybody in your office, including Lieutenant Simons, and I made sure the print cards I used were the cards from when they were hired. All were official SFPD cards."

"All right, Steve. Thanks. I appreciate your help, and please don't mention this to anyone. Keep it between us, okay?"

"You kidding? My career, and probably my life, would be over if anyone found out what we are doing. So, if you need anything else, let me know," he said.

"I will, Steve. Thanks."

Vince went back to his office and sat at his desk. Twenty minutes later, he was still there, his head in his hands, deep in thought, when Clark came up to him and asked if he was okay.

"Yeah, Mike. Hey. let's take a ride. I need to talk to you in private."

"That doesn't sound good, but, okay, let's go."

Vince drove up 3rd Street, crossed Market then turned left on Geary, and drove past Union Square. As he drove, he told Clark what he had Jacobs do.

"So you suspected one of us was the killer? Including me?"

"No, Mike. I had a feeling it was someone in our office, so I had Jacobs check everyone as a precaution. You know I would never think that of you."

"Gee, thanks, Vince." Clark grinned at him and said, "It's okay, I'm just pulling your chain a bit. I would have done the same thing. Besides, what would you have thought if you didn't have my prints run, and Jacobs came up empty? No, Vince, it was the right thing to do. So, now that you've got that out of your system, where do we go from here?"

"That's what I want to talk to you about. We keep doing what we are, with the surveillance crew, and working all the leads we have, but you and I are gonna start looking a little deeper."

"What do we do?"

"First, I'm still not convinced our killer isn't in this office."

Clark sighed. "Geez, Vince! What does it take? You've had all our prints run, you've got nothing but a hunch on this, and you won't let it go. We need to get busy and catch this guy, not chase shadows based on your hunches."

"Mike, how long have we been working together? Four, five years? You know I don't waste my time chasing hunches. I know, Mike, deep down inside, our killer is close to us. If not in the office, then very closely linked to us. I have an idea, but I need more info. When the time comes, I need to know I can count on you. Can I, Mike?"

"Of course, Vince. So, what do you have in mind?"

Vince pulled into the parking lot of the Presidio Golf Course and parked. "I'm not sure just yet, but you will know when I decide what to do. I'll keep you informed."

"I don't like the sound of that, Vince. I'm your partner. Don't you feel comfortable enough with me, or trust me enough to confide in me?"

"It's not that, Mike. I still don't have a good idea of what to do. I need to think on this a while. Like you said, maybe I'm chasing shadows, going at this the wrong way. I just need a few days to sort all this out. Trust me, Mike. You will be the first to know."

"All right, Vince. I'll give you a few more days to work this out, but then, we need to get back to basics."

"You got it, partner." Vince started the car and drove out of the lot, heading back toward the office. They didn't talk all the way back. When they arrived, Vince found the forensics report from the Sausalito Police Department on his desk. Cullin was sitting at Clark's desk, working on the computer, trying to identify other possible targets of the killer. When he saw Vince and Clark walk in, he rushed over, waving a sheet of paper.

"Vince! I think I got something. I found a parolee that may be our next victim."

Vince took off his coat and hung it on the back of his chair. "Who is it?"

"A guy named Willie Desmond. Black male, 34 years old. Was released on parole from Folsom Prison last week after nine years inside for murder, second degree."

"Who'd he kill that makes him so special?"

"A nun, Sister Ann Marie. She disappeared 13 years ago from the convent at Saint Michaels Church in the Sunset District. Found her body seven months later in a shallow grave near Land's End, minus her head, which has never been found."

"What makes this so special? Was there a sexual assault? Any evidence of torture? Devil worship? Anything like that?" Vince asked, leaning back in his chair.

"Well, no, but decapitating a nun? I would think that is pretty bad, killing a servant of God."

"Yeah, it is, but it doesn't really fit our profile very well. All right, to be safe, let's assign one of the officers to him. Where does he live?"

Cullin found the address on the parole sheet. "1712 Ortega." Cullin looked up and said, "The rotten bastard moved back into the Sunset! Can you believe that?"

"Always happens that way, Robbie," Clark said. "They always seem to find their way back, never get too far away from their roots."

Vince smiled ruefully. "They always come back," he said, shaking his head slowly side to side.

Clark interrupted. "We'll have to pull someone off another surveillance, Vince. Everyone but you is assigned to someone."

"I don't want to do that, so I'll take this Desmond guy, at least until we can cut someone loose. Give me the info, Robbie. I'll start tonight."

***

Later that night, Vince was parked on the street just up from Desmond's rooming house, watching his windows. He could see the flickering of a television set through the thin curtains, and every once in a while, a shadow would pass by. He looked at his watch and saw it was 11:38 p.m. Looking back up at Desmond's window, he saw the flickering light go out. He watched the dark window for ten more minutes, then said, "Fuck this!" and started up the car. He drove away, knowing that Desmond was in for the night. Muttering to himself, he drove toward the office. The radio had been quiet all night.

A few blocks from his office, he decided to drive over to Clark's location, see if he could convince him to meet at Red's Java Hut on the Embarcadero, south of Market Street, for coffee at the end of the shift. Vince turned off Bush Street onto Octavia, and pulled up next to Clark's car, parked near Lafayette Park. He shut off his lights as Clark got out and walked over to him. Vince rolled down the window, letting the cold wind in. Clark leaned down and said, "Quit a bit early, did we?"

"Yeah. Desmond is sleeping, and I think it's a long shot our guy will go after him. Everything quiet here?"

"Yeah. My guy hasn't left his room all night. Lights went out about an hour and a half ago."

"Wanna meet me at Red's, get some coffee?"

"Sure. I'll see you there in about a half hour."

"Good. See you then."

***

The killer drove slowly on California Street and turned right on Octavia. He was excited about what he was going to do. *Time for you to pay for your crime,* he thought. He knew the plan, and it was flawless. Nothing could go wrong. The streets were deserted, just like he was told they would be. It was going to be easy. He began whistling along with the radio. As he made the turn, he saw Inspector Clark's car was still parked where it had been when he drove by earlier, but Clark was out of the vehicle and standing by another car stopped next to him, talking to the driver. He couldn't see who was in the other car, and that worried him. It had the look of an unmarked police car, but he didn't know for sure. He put on his brakes, stopping several car lengths back, and stared into the night, losing his sense of confidence. The warning bells began going off in his head, and he put the van in reverse, starting to backing up.

Torelli and Clark both looked at the van as it approached them from behind. Clark turned back to Vince. "Here comes a van, Vince. Better move. I'll meet you at the coffee shop."

Clark straightened up and started walking back to his car as Vince looked in his rear view mirror. He saw the van start to reverse quickly, causing its tires to squeal as the driver accelerated, backing away from him. He remembered the van he saw leaving the alley when Sachs was kidnapped from the video store, and the other stolen vans the killer used, causing him to become alarmed enough to want to check it out.

"Clark! Get in the car. Hurry! That may be our suspect leaving."

"What? Where?"

"Just get in the car," Vince shouted.

Clark sprinted to the passenger side and jumped in, slamming the door as Vince reversed quickly down Octavia. Vince lost site of the van as it backed to the right around the corner onto California Street. He and Clark drew their pistols as he accelerated, spinning the wheel as they entered the intersection, causing the car to slide around the corner. Vince slammed on the brakes, stopping the car. As he jammed the gear selector in drive, he realized he was facing the van head on.

The killer stomped on the gas pedal, spinning the van's tires, causing blue smoke to pour from underneath. He drove directly at their car, crashing head-on into the sedan, pushing it backwards several feet. His seat belt kept him from being injured, and because he was braced for the collision, he suffered no ill effects. He jammed the gear selector into reverse and backed the van away from Vince's car, which was leaking fluid from the smashed radiator. He backed up 50 feet, slammed the lever into drive and accelerated towards Vince's car again, smashing into the right front headlight, spinning the car 180 degrees. He stomped on the accelerator, again spinning the tires, the engine now smoking. Three blocks later, He slowed the van to the speed limit, made a quick right, a left, and another right, and pulled over to the curb. The driver looked around and saw there was no one on the street, no vehicles driving by, and the houses were all dark. He sat back in the seat, taking deep breaths, trying to slow his racing heart. After a few minutes, he got out of the smoking van and casually walked away, limping slightly.

When Vince spun the car around the corner, intending to speed after the van, he was surprised to see it accelerating toward him. He and Clark both raised their pistols, but before they could fire, the van smashed into the front of the car. Clark was thrown forward into the windshield, cracking it with his head, knocking him unconscious.

Vince struck the steering wheel with his chest, knocking the wind out of him, wrenching his right shoulder, and causing him to drop his pistol on the floor by his feet. Before he could recover his breath, the van backed up and crashed into the car again, spinning it around. He looked at the van as it passed, but was unable to see the driver. He heard the sound of the van accelerating past him down the street. He sat up and slowly opened the door, getting out of the car with difficulty, staggering around to the passenger side. Gasping for breath, Vince pulled open the door, using his left hand, catching Clark as his body started to fall sideways out of the vehicle. The effort made his shoulder flare with pain. He sat on the ground next to the open door, gently cradling Clark across his lap. He could see he was breathing, though he was still unconscious. He could see Clark's pistol on the floorboard of the car and reached inside, picking it up. He held the gun in his left hand, ready to protect himself and Clark if the suspect returned.

A crowd had started to gather around the wrecked, smoking car. Vince looked around, shouting "SFPD", flashing the weapon. He pointed at one of the bystanders and said, "You, go call 9-1-1. Tell them there is an officer down at this location and you need an ambulance and backup."

"Yessir," a young Latino said, running across the street to his house. Vince turned back to Clark, saying, "Hold on, Buddy. Help is on the way."

***

Liz Maltby saw the crowd gathered around the car as she turned onto the street. She pulled to the curb and quickly got out, cursing softly to herself, calling to her cameraman to grab his camera and follow her. They ran to the wrecked car where Liz began telling the cameraman what to photograph. She saw Vince kneeling by the open passenger door, holding Clark's hand, as Clark began to regain consciousness, moaning softly, rolling his bloody head side to side. The cameraman took several shots as Liz walked up to Vince and asked if there was anything she could do.

Vince looked up at her. "What the hell are you doing here?"

"Looking for a story. What on earth happened here?"

"Had a bit of an accident. Here comes the ambulance. You better get out of the way, and get that fucking photographer outta here!" Vince shouted, grimacing with pain from his bruised shoulder.

"All right, all right! C'mon, Eddy, let's go." She turned on her heels and walked toward her car. *God-damn it! There goes my big story. The stupid shit. What a fuck up!*

***

Vince followed the paramedics as they wheeled Clark to the ambulance and slid the stretcher inside. He climbed in and sat on the bench.

"What do you think you're doing?" the paramedic asked.

"Going with him."

"Not before we take a look at you. Outside of the bruise on your cheek, where does it hurt?"

"My shoulder. Hurts like hell when I move it, and my chest. Hurts a bit when I breathe."

"Let me take a look," the paramedic said, gently feeling Vince's right shoulder. He placed one hand on the joint, grabbed Vince's elbow with his other hand, and said, "I'm gonna rotate your shoulder a bit, see what the damage is. Let me know when the pain gets to be too much."

He gently rotated Vince's arm in a circle, until Vince grunted in pain, saying, "That's about as far as it'll go."

"Well, doesn't feel like it's broken, and it's not dis-located. I'll immobilize it, and we'll get some x-rays at the hospital, but I think it's just a bad bruise."

The ride to the hospital seemed to take forever. Vince leaned back against the side of the ambulance, watching Clark, who had lapsed back into unconsciousness. Every bump in the road sent a jolt of pain shooting through his shoulder. He cradled his right arm with his other arm, pulling it in to his chest to try and stabilize the injured shoulder. He closed his eyes and rested his head against the wall. His whole body ached and he had started to shiver from shock. The paramedic riding in the back of the ambulance must have noticed, as he took a blanket out of his seat compartment and draped it over Vince. Vince opened his eyes and smiled slightly, grateful for the warmth.

X-rays revealed Vince's shoulder was not broken, but had been sprained and badly bruised. Maggie had arrived a half hour after he got to the hospital, and was sitting in a chair in the examination room, watching him, the worry lines etched on her face. "Use the sling for the next week, Inspector," the nurse instructed. "After that, you can take it off, but limit how much you use the arm. No heavy lifting for at least two weeks." Turning to Maggie, she said, "Can you make sure he doesn't use that shoulder too soon?"

"Count on it, Nurse."

Turning back to Vince, she said, "I can give you a prescription for some pain killers if you want it."

"No, thanks. I'll take some Tylenol or Advil if I need it."

"Tell you what, I'll get you that prescription anyway, then if the Advil or Tylenol doesn't work, you can get it filled. Anything else I can do for you?"

"Can I see my partner?" Vince asked, as Maggie helped him put on his shirt and buttoned it for him.

The nurse helped him put on the sling. "Sure. He's gonna be fine. I'll take you there."

Clark was lying in the hospital bed, his head heavily bandaged. Sandy, his wife, was standing next to the bed holding his hand. Her eyes were red and swollen from crying. A doctor was standing at the foot of the bed, writing on a chart.

"How's he doing, Doc?" Vince whispered, afraid of disturbing Clark, who appeared to be sleeping. Clark's right leg was immobilized with an air cast, and an I.V. dripped slowly into his arm.

"Oh, Inspector Torelli," the doctor said, looking up at him. Speaking in hushed tones he said, "He'll be fine. He's got a nasty gash on his scalp and a concussion, but no skull fracture. Took a few stitches to close it. His right leg is broken, but other than that, and a few other bruises, he's allright."

"Is he awake?"

"He was, but he's sleeping now. We'll set the leg and cast it in the morning, when we're sure his concussion isn't serious and the swelling goes down a bit. We'll keep him here for a couple of days, to keep an eye on him, but he should be able to go home then, and should fully recover."

"Good news, Doc." He turned to Sandy. "Is there anything I can do?

"No, thanks, Vince." She wiped her eyes with a crumpled Kleenex. "I'm going to spend the night here. I don't want him to wake up alone. Allie is with my mother, so I'm all set."

"If you're sure."

"I am, thanks. You go home. Get some rest."

"I will. Tell Mike I'll be in to see him tomorrow, when he wakes up."

Vince walked over and gingerly hugged her, then walked out of the room, Maggie following.

***

Once at home, Vince poured a shot of Jack Daniel's, sat on the couch and turned the television on. He leaned back and sipped the whiskey, feeling its warmth spread through his body as he swallowed it. Maggie came in and sat next to him, taking his hand in hers. "Let's go to bed, Babe. You need your rest."

"I'll be there in a few minutes. I'm too keyed up to sleep. I think I'll watch a little television first."

"OK, Honey. Don't stay up too late." Maggie stood up, turned to face him and took his face in both hands. "I love you," she said, softly, kissing him on the forehead. She turned and walked out of the room.

Vince finished his drink a few minutes later. Combined with the alcohol, the stress and fatigue had wiped him out. Stifling a huge yawn, he walked toward the bedroom. As he passed his youngest son's room, he went in stood at the foot of his bed, just watching him sleep. He then went into his oldest son's room and did the same.

He would often do this at particularly difficult times. It served to remind him why he worked so hard at his job, why he took the risks he did. The more evil he took off the streets, the safer it would be for everyone, especially his family. This wasn't the first time he had been injured on the job, and he knew it probably wouldn't be the last. As he did each time he watched his sons sleep, he vowed to always do the best he could to protect them. Feeling better, he made his way to his bedroom.

Chapter 23

Vince's whole body ached when he tried to get out of bed the next morning. He groaned with the effort, and sat back down on the mattress. His shoulder felt like it was on fire, and his neck and back were stiff.

"Jesus. I feel like hammered shit!" he mumbled, settling back in bed.

"That good, huh?" Maggie said, as she came into the room, carrying a cup of coffee. "Today you just rest. Stay in bed. I brought you some coffee, so if you can manage to sit up, I'll give it to you. Are you hungry? Want me to make some breakfast?"

"Coffee sounds good. Just some toast, okay? I'm not too hungry."

"All right. I already called the office for you and told them you wouldn't be in."

Vince started to protest, but she cut him off. "No arguments. Today you rest, and maybe, the operative word being maybe, you can go in for a little while tomorrow. Here's some Advil. It will help with the pain. I'll be right back, and yes, I will bring the paper."

Maggie left the room and he soon heard her moving about the kitchen. He took the Advil with the last of his coffee, and slid down in bed, trying to get as comfortable as he could. He closed his eyes, willing the pain to go away, and fell asleep to the sound of Maggie humming to the radio.

***

The killer, too, awoke to an aching body. His knee was swollen, and he had a slight limp when he walked. He tested it, finding he could walk without a limp with a bit of effort and some pain, but knew it would be a day or two before he could walk normally. His lip was sore where he had bitten it during the crash, drawing blood. He knew he couldn't go to work like that. It would give him away, so he called his boss and made up a story about his sister in Bakersfield having fallen and broken her leg, and that he needed to go down there for a couple of days to care for her. He poured a cup of coffee and sat at the table, thinking about what had happened the night before. He knew he had been lucky. It could have been him that got the worst of the crash. He could be in custody, being questioned by Torelli. He would have to be more careful from here on.

Damn Torelli! he thought. *He's always messing up my plans. How can he always be in the right place at the right time? How does he know? How much does he suspect?*

He stood up and started pacing through the dining room, practicing walking without a limp, thinking more and more about Torelli, getting more and more agitated. As he walked, his knee loosened up and before long, he was able to walk normally. After a couple of minutes, he picked up the phone and dialed a number.

***

Lieutenant Simons called Vince later that morning. Maggie answered the phone, telling him to hold on while she checked to see if he was awake.

When she saw he was, she asked if he felt liked taking the phone call. He nodded and reached for the phone.

"Hey, Boss."

"How ya doing, Vince?" Simons asked. "Ya feeling all right?"

"I'm okay, just sore. Doctor told me to take it easy today. I'll be back tomorrow."

"No, you won't," Maggie said from the doorway. Raising her voice, she said, "And don't you encourage him, Len. He needs to rest."

"You hear that, Boss?"

"Yep. Guess we better do as she says, huh?"

"Yeah. You don't want to face the wrath of Maggie," Vince said, grinning at her as she leaned against the doorframe, her arms crossed over her chest. She smiled at him, blew him a kiss, turned and walked from the room.

"How's Clark doing?" Vince asked.

"He'll be fine. I talked with him this morning, and he's resting comfortably. Gonna have to stay in the hospital for a couple more days. He's sore all over, but there's no permanent damage. Sandy told me the doctor said his leg will heal as good as new. He should be back on light duty within a month."

"That's good news. Anything going on with the investigation?"

"Yeah. We found the van last night a few blocks away, abandoned. We had it towed to the impound yard, and the forensics guys are going over it with a fine toothed comb. Print guys already did their job. Got lots of prints, so they're running them thru the system now. Maybe we'll get lucky and get a hit."

"That would be nice, but I doubt we'll get anything useful. I'll bet the van was stolen, probably from either San Francisco or Oakland airport, and the only prints you'll find will be the owner's."

"You're probably right. The van belongs to a local delivery company. They park their vehicles at the long-term lot at SFO. They didn't know it was missing until we called them this morning. The van was last used two days ago, and had been parked there around one in the afternoon. The company wouldn't have known it was missing until this morning. Hey, how'd you know that? You psychic or something?"

"Yeah. Or something. Anything else?"

"We found a couple of witnesses who saw what happened. They've been interviewed, so between them and you, we've got a pretty good idea of the events. Only thing, though, no one got a look at the driver. Too dark."

"Figures. Just our luck. Damn it, we need a break."

"I've got the whole squad working overtime on this. It got personal when he tried to kill a couple of my guys. We'll get him, Vince. You rest, take tomorrow off, and come back when you're ready. If anything else breaks, I'll let you know."

"Thanks, Boss."

"All right, Vince. Talk to you later."

Vince called the hospital to talk to Clark, but was told he was getting his leg properly set and casted, and would not be taking phone calls. Vince asked that Clark be told he had called, and the operator said she would leave him a message.

***

The next day, Vince was able to get out of bed without too much pain, though it took him awhile to work out the stiffness. His shoulder was very sore, and when he looked at himself in the bathroom mirror, he saw the deep purple bruising and black eye on his face. He smiled and gingerly probed the bruise, wincing in pain. He put his sling on and went into the kitchen for coffee.

"How you feeling this morning?" Maggie asked, sitting across from him.

"Better. Still sore, though. Like the way I look?"

"Absolutely. You look like Stallone after the first Rocky movie, only sexier."

"Oh, yeah," he said, leering at her. "Where's the boys?"

"Don't get any ideas, big boy! They're off to school. I threatened them with massive amounts of yard work if they bothered you this morning. What are you up to today?"

"Not much. I'd like to go see Clark at the hospital. Then maybe stop by the office for a little while, check on how the case is going."

"I don't want you doing too much, Vince. You are not ready to go back to work yet," Maggie said, as she adjusted the sling on his arm, frowning.

"I know, Babe. I promise, I'll only be there an hour. I promise."

"All right. I've got to get to work. You able to drive?"

"Yeah. I'm gonna finish the paper, then go. I should be home by noon."

"Okay. No later than noon, Vince," she admonished him. "Love you."

Chapter 24

Three days later, Vince was back at work, and Clark had been released from the hospital. Vince got in the habit of taking the sling off as soon as he was out of sight of his house, so Maggie wouldn't see, and though his shoulder was still sore, he had almost full movement back.

He was reading through the witness statements from the scene, and though the witnesses couldn't describe the driver of the van in detail, two of them got the impression the driver was in his mid-to-late thirties, and had thinning hair. One witness described his hair as almost blonde, while the other said he was a brunette. They could not provide any distinctive features of the driver's face.

The forensics team had been over the van with a fine-toothed comb. All the prints found had been identified as belonging to employees of the delivery company, but a very small droplet of blood had been located on the steering wheel. The blood was collected for typing and DNA analysis for comparison when a suspect was located. Vacuuming the van revealed dozens of fibers and other detritus, none of which would be of value to the investigation.

"Hey, Jensen," he called across the room. "Any chance of finding a witness where the van was dumped?"

"Nope. We did a pretty thorough canvas of the neighborhood. No one saw or heard anything."

"Would it do any good to send another team to re-canvas?"

"We could try, but we already talked to most everybody on the street."

"Why don't we give it a try? Send a couple of the patrol guys assigned to us. Have them talk to everyone. If someone isn't home, I want to know their name and when they will be back."

"Okay, Vince. I'll get right on it."

As Vince was finishing with Jensen, Cullin walked in the room, and made a beeline to Vince.

"Hey, Vince! Glad to see you're back. How are you feeling? Shoulder better?" he said, gently pumping Vince's hand.

"I'm all right, Robbie, thanks. Any more on the Machado killing?"

"No. The water washed away any evidence on the body and the clothing, though I doubt there was any to begin with. Sausalito police are baffled with this one. More than willing to turn it over to us as part of our investigation."

"Good. It's definitely linked. Anything come out of our surveillance the last couple of nights?"

"All quiet. Maybe our suspect got a bit banged up in the crash, too. Might be a bit under the weather."

"One can only hope, Robbie. The team ready for tonight?"

"Yeah. Lieutenant Simons pulled one of the patrol guys off one of the least likely targets and has him watching Clark's guy. It's been quiet the last couple of days."

"I don't think it will last. The killer is going to want to let us know he is still active, and still in charge. We'll have to be alert for the next few days."

"Are you going out tonight?"

"No, not for a couple of more nights. It's gonna take a few days for this shoulder to heal completely, so I'm going to spend some time at home. But, I've left orders to be called right away if anything happens."

Cullin looked at his watch. "Oh, crap. I've got a meeting with my boss in five minutes." He grabbed his coat off the chair. "See you at the briefing this afternoon."

Vince watched him walk away, then picked up the phone and dialed Liz Maltby's number.

"Hey, Liz, It's Vince. We need to talk. Can you meet me? Good, I'll be there in thirty minutes." Vince hung up, grabbed his coat, and walked out of the room, taking the elevator down to the garage.

Liz hung up the phone after talking with Vince. She stared at the phone for a few moments, then grabbed her cell phone and dialed a number. When her call was answered, she said, in a half whisper, "He called me, said we had to talk. We're meeting in a half hour in Union Square. No, I don't think he suspects anything. Yes, I will be careful, don't worry. What happened the other night? I got there right when you said I should. I know it was fucked up! I was there. Well, whoever's fault it was, it screwed me out of an exclusive. Look, you promised I could be there when the next one was grabbed. I'm going to hold you to that. All right, I'll call you after I talk to Torelli." Liz hung up the phone, looking around to make sure no one was within earshot.

She is becoming a problem I don't need, he thought, as he hung up.

***

Vince walked up the grass at Union Square, and saw Liz sitting on a bench. He walked over to her and sat down. Several people were walking around the square, heading to their favorite lunch spots. Others were lounging on the grass and benches, eating or reading. The usual tourists were wandering around, going in and out of the stores, window shopping, doing what tourists usually do in San Francisco.

He looked straight ahead. "I am really interested in your reason for being at the scene the other night. And before you start talking, I'm not buying your 'just a coincidence' excuse."

"What are you implying, Vince? We did just happen to be in the area. We were heading back to the office when I saw all the cop cars. I am a reporter, you know. I was curious, so we followed the cops."

Vince turned and looked at her, not saying anything for a while, just studying her face. "I don't believe you, Liz. I think you know more than you're telling me. If I'm right, then you have information that could lead to us finding this psycho. I would hope you aren't so career driven that you would withhold that information. If you are, I'll send you to prison, I promise you that." He stood up and turned to face her. "You think about it, Liz. Think real hard. You've got 24 hours. I'll be in touch."

As Vince turned and walked away, she stood up. "Vince, wait! I'm telling the truth!"

Vince continued walking, ignoring her. She watched him walk away, hands on her hips, silently cursing to herself. She walked toward her car, and got in, seething with anger. She tried several times to call Torelli and finally gave up when he didn't answer. Finally, she dialed another number. "Its me. Don't talk, just listen. Torelli is on to me. He knows. How the hell do I know? He figured it out somehow. No, I did not tell him anything yet. That's what I said, yet. He told me I have 24 hours to think it over, and then he will arrest me for conspiracy and accessory if I don't tell him the truth. No, I haven't made up my mind. What do you mean he's bluffing? How do you know? Well, I'm not so sure. I'm not gonna do anything until tomorrow. Yes, I know. I'll call you in the morning with my decision." She disconnected the call and put the phone in her purse.

He shut off his phone and placed it in his pocket. *Time to take care of a loose end,* he thought. *Too bad, I was beginning to like her.* He thought for a moment, then took out his cell phone and dialed.

Chapter 25

Vince took off his coat and hung it over the back of his chair, then walked over to Cullin. "Anything new, Robbie?"

"Not yet, Vince. How're you doing?"

"I'm okay. Still a bit sore, but almost back to a hundred percent. Listen, Robbie, with Clark out of the picture for a while, I'm gonna have to rely more on you. I'll need you to do some of the stuff Clark was doing. That means you'll be taking a more active roll. Is that okay with you?"

"Of course it is, Vince. Just tell me what you want me to do." Cullin slid forward on his chair, leaning in toward Torelli. His face lit up as Vince told him what he would be doing, and a grin spread across his face. He was obviously thrilled that he was being given more responsibility, even though it was mostly making phone calls and doing computer searches.

An hour later, Vince called the fingerprint tech to see if he had identified the print from Sach's body. He was told there was no new information, and unless he had something new, it was a dead end. There was nowhere else to look for a match.

***

At ten forty-five that night, Liz Maltby left O'Rielly's Pub on Harrison Street near the Embarcadero. She'd had several drinks while sitting alone at the bar, thinking about what she was going to tell Torelli.

She decided her best course of action was to tell the truth. She had written down the cell phone number for the killer, and jotted down several things about him she knew that might help identify him. She ignored several attempts by men in the bar to engage her in conversation, and sat quietly, looking at the notes she had made. At one point, she crumpled the paper in her hand, and started to throw it into a waste basket behind the bar, but stopped before she released it. She placed the crumpled paper on the bar and smoothed it with her hands, then folded it in half, then half again, and placed it in the pocket of her pants. Finishing her drink, she left the bar and walked up Harrison toward her car parked two blocks away, dialing her phone.

"Hi, Vince. It's Liz. Look, I want to meet with you tomorrow. I've got some information for you that might help in your investigation."

"Okay,where and when?"

"I'll meet you at Union Square again, about 11:30? I'll be at the same bench as today."

"I'll be waiting. And, Liz? I will only accept full disclosure. That's the only way you might be able to avoid going to prison, understand?"

"Yes, goddamn it. I will tell you everything in the morning."

She disconnected the call and quickened her pace up the street, pulling her coat collar up to protect her from the chill of the damp San Francisco night.

***

He watched her talking on her cell phone as she walked toward the van. He had parked it on the same side of the street, a half block from her car. He was standing behind the van, waiting for her, wearing black sweat pants, a black sweatshirt, and a black ski cap, which he pulled down over his face as she got near, leaving only his eyes exposed. The streetlights were far apart and the usual fog had flowed over the city, diffusing their light.

She had her head down as she passed the van, not paying attention to the street, and he quickly moved behind her, swinging the lead filled leather sap at her head. The sap struck her just behind the right ear with a solid "thunk", knocking her unconscious immediately.

He caught her as she fell and lowered her to the ground, looking around to see if anyone was nearby. There was no one on the sidewalk, and the street was clear of cars. He pulled the ski mask off, placing it inside his sweatshirt. He placed his hands under her arms and half lifted, half dragged her to the back of the van. He had her halfway in when a car turned onto Harrison from Spear Street, briefly illuminating them with its headlights. He stood in front of her body, pulling the door partially closed to block the car's view, waiting until it passed. He watched the car as it drove down Harrison and turned right onto the Embarcadero, apparently unaware of what was going on.

He wiped the sudden sweat from his brow, and quickly pushed Liz the rest of the way into the van. Closing the doors, he ran around to the driver's door and got in. He took several deep calming breaths, then started the motor and drove slowly down Harrison.

***

It had been almost a week since the accident and Clark was getting around with the use of crutches. He hobbled his way into the kitchen and sat at the table as Vince walked in, followed by Sandy. His leg stuck straight out due to the cast, and Sandy moved one of the kitchen chairs so he could rest his leg on it.

"Hey, Partner," he said. "How goes the battle?"

Vince smiled as he sat opposite him. "Slowly, Mike, very slowly. Hey, Sandy says you've been a real pain in the ass. Says she's gonna hire a nurse to come in, and she's moving to a hotel for a couple of weeks."

"Vince! You cut me to the quick! The truth is, I'm not getting nearly enough attention around here."

Sandy, at the counter pouring them coffee, muttered, "Oh, God." She turned, carrying the cups, and, winking at Vince, said, "You know him, Vince. He's such a baby! Always whining about his leg hurting, wanting me to feed him, comfort him, 'Get me my medicine, my leg hurts, can I have another pillow'. Jesus! Can I come stay with you and Maggie?"

Vince laughed as much at what she was saying as the goofy grin on Clark's face. "Anytime, Sandy."

"See, Vince, see how she treats me, her poor, injured husband? I get no sympathy," Clark said, as Sandy leaned over and kissed the top of his head.

"I'm sure, Mike," he said, shaking his head.

"Seriously, Vince, how's your shoulder?"

"Back to normal. Got full movement back, and no pain. When can you come back to work?"

"Doc said it would be another few days, then I can return to light duty. That means office work. Yuck! If anything will make me heal faster, it's being assigned to desk duty. Anything new on the case?"

"Maybe. It's encouraging that he hasn't struck again. It had been almost a week with nothing. Maybe he got a bit banged up, too. By the way, I'm meeting that reporter, Liz Maltby in a couple of hours. I think she's got something for me that will break the case."

"Really? What is it?"

"I don't know, but whatever it is, it's gotta help. I met with her yesterday and told her I knew she had information she was holding back, that I would charge her as an accomplice if she didn't come forward."

"You got enough to back it up?"

"Nope, just wanted to lean on her a bit. I have my suspicions. You how she is, Mike, what our history is, so I wouldn't put anything past her."

"What did she say?"

"Nothing, just had this startled look on her face. Confirmed my suspicions that she does know something."

"Why did you suspect her?"

"I just can't rationalize why she was at the scene of our crash so quickly. She said she was just in the area and saw all the cop cars rolling and followed them, but that just didn't sound right. She's been at all the body dumps, and told me she's been getting phone calls from the killer, tipping her off. Said it was because he wanted her to print his story. I think she's made some sort of deal with him, and can give us something that may lead to him."

"Like what?"

"I don't know. Maybe a location where she meets him, a description of him or his vehicle, a cell phone number, something."

"God, I hope so. What time are you meeting her?"

"Eleven thirty. Speaking of which, I've got to get going." Vince looked at his watch, then stood up and shook Clark's hand, leaning over to give him a quick hug. "Don't get up, Mike, I know my way out."

"Very funny, Vince. Call me as soon as you know anything new," Clark said, as Vince walked from the room.

***

He had stripped her naked and tied her to the chair in the trailer as she slept off the pills he had given her earlier, telling her, when she had regained consciousness, that they were Tylenol and would help ease the pain from the blow to her head. He stood back, admiring her, feeling a stirring in his groin he hadn't felt in a long time. *No!* he thought, *she's just like the others. Quit looking at her that way. She's just a piece of meat.* He shuddered, shook his head to clear his thoughts then walked out of the trailer. Just as he closed the door, her cell phone rang, muffled by her clothing stuffed in the plastic bag on the floor of the warehouse.

Chapter 26

At 11:30, Vince was sitting on the bench in Union Square, waiting for Liz to show up. He waited for a half hour then tried her cell phone, getting her voice mail. "Liz, where are you? I sure hope you aren't planning on not meeting me. Call me. I'll be waiting."

After another half hour, and two more unsuccessful calls to her cell Vince muttered, "Goddamn her!" then stood up and walked quickly to his car. As he unlocked the driver's door, he saw a business card under the windshield. He pulled it free. It was one of Liz Maltby's cards. He turned it over, then froze. In black writing it said, *Your meeting has been cancelled. The R.K.*

"Shit!" Vince cried, then jumped in the driver's seat, and raced from the area. As he drove back towards the office, he called Cullin's cell phone. "Robbie? It's Vince. He's got Liz Maltby. Who? Who else! The killer! I was supposed to meet her and she didn't show up. I found a note from him on my car. Yes, I'm sure. I'll be in the office in a few minutes. Where are you? Okay, let your boss know, then get over there. Get the task force members together. I'm pulling them off the babysitting detail. We're gonna get back to basics. See you in a few."

A half hour later Vince paced back and forth in front of the task force. When he had gotten back to the office, he immediately took the small evidence envelop containing the business card to the crime lab to be checked for fingerprints, and a possible handwriting analysis, though the killer had written the note in felt tip pen. "Anybody got any ideas that might help us figure out how this guy knew she was meeting me?"

Cullin looked around at the other officers and detectives, who were shaking their heads and muttering. "Maybe she called him and told him about the meeting," he said, sipping from a soda can.

"God, I hope she wasn't that dumb. If she did, she signed her own death warrant."

"So what do we do now, Vince?" Cullin said, tossing the empty can into the wastebasket next to the desk.

"We go looking for him. We're gonna blanket this city, look in every logical place we can think of until we find him. We're going hunting, ladies and gentlemen! I want everyone ready to go by four o'clock. Meet back here, and bring flashlights and jackets. We may be out late tonight. Oh, yeah. Make sure you all have your ballistic vests with you. This guy is dangerous, so don't get complacent or underestimate him. See you this afternoon."

As the others left the office, Vince went to Lt. Simons door, knocked then entered. He spent the next fifteen minutes updating him on the case and explaining his plan.

"If we can find where the murders are taking place, we can find him. We will be canvassing the dock area south of Market. I'm sure it's somewhere down there."

"What makes you think that, Vince? Seems to me we don't have much information to indicate that."

"We don't, Boss, but I got a hunch I can't shake. The forensics crew found mud with a high salt content on one of the victims, and creosote on others. Sounds like a dock to me."

"C'mon, Vince," Lieutenant Simons said, shaking his head. "That could be anywhere in the city. All we got is salty mud, and creosote soaked land. You gotta have more than that."

"Just trust me, Boss. I know I'm right." Looking at his watch, Vince said, "I gotta make some calls. Are we done here?"

"Yeah, yeah. Get going."

As Vince opened the office door lieutenant Simons said, "You better be right about this, Vince."

"I am, Boss. You'll see."

When he got back to his desk, he saw that most everyone had left, including Cullin. He retrieved the empty soda can Cullin had thrown in the trash, placing it in a plastic bag. He wrote Cullin's name on it and dropped it into a large paper sack. He collected the other cans and paper coffee cups left around the room by the other task force officers, placing each in a similar plastic bag and writing their name on it. All the cans and cups went into the paper sack, which Vince stapled shut and placed in his bottom desk drawer. He then called Forensic Services and asked for Steve Jacobs.

"Steve? It's Torelli. I need another favor. I got a bunch of cans and paper cups I need you to print. Anything you find I want you to compare with the print found on Sach's body. Yeah, the one we couldn't identify. No, there won't be a request for latent print identification with it. I need you to do this without anyone knowing. I know, I know, it is irregular, and yes, both our asses will be in a sling if anyone finds out, but it is important. Thanks, Steve, I owe you big time. That's fine. Whenever you can spare the time. Just don't take too long, okay? Yeah, I love you, too. I'll be there in a couple of minutes. Thanks."

Vince hung up the phone, took the paper sack out of his desk drawer, and left the room.

***

Three hours later, Vince was waiting for the rest of the task force to show up to begin the briefing, when Cullin approached him. "Will you be needing me for the briefing, Vince?"

"No, Robbie. I'm just gonna go over a few things with the guys and get them out on the street. There's nothing going on you don't already know about."

"If it's all right, I'm going to take off. I'm kinda tired today. Gonna go home, eat a T.V. dinner, then crash."

"You have been working a lot lately. Go ahead. I'll call you if anything breaks."

"Thanks, Vince. See you in the morning. You be careful tonight."

"I will. G'nite, Robbie."

When the rest of the task force arrived and settled down, Vince began the briefing.

"We're not gonna be babysitting anyone tonight. What we're gonna do is pair up and do a thorough search of the waterfront. We're looking for the location of the murders. I believe all the victims were murdered at the same place, then taken to the dumpsites. We find that place, we find our killer.

We're gonna concentrate on the area along Embarcadero south of the Ferry Building, all the way to 5th Street."

The group began grumbling among themselves, realizing they had a large area to canvass and that they would be out until the early morning hours.

"I know, I know," Vince said, holding his hands up, palms out. "That's a lot of area to cover. We can narrow it down somewhat, though. Concentrate on abandoned buildings on both sides of the street. Look for places that are out of the way, off the main drag. Places where no one is likely to go, or to be noticed going there. Here's where we'll be looking," he said, as he stood up and made his way to a large map tacked to the wall. "We will start here," he said, placing a red pushpin on it, "And end up here," placing another red pin at the intersection of Embarcadero and Fifth Street. "Make sure you shake the doors, try the windows, and whatever else you need to do to see inside, other than causing damage. Look carefully, people. Anything that seems unusual needs to be documented. Okay, pair up."

Once they had selected their partners, Vince moved among them, assigning them a number and recording their names, until he had a complete list. The area Vince had them searching was run-down, with few businesses still open. Most of the warehouses had gone out of business years earlier, and the docks had started sagging due to old age, having been built in the early nineteen hundreds. The area was mostly deserted. Slated for renovation, the City had not yet allocated the money, nor secured additional funding for the redevelopment. Most of the tenants had been forced to leave due to safety code or fire code violations, and some of the buildings had been abandoned for more than a year. There were few streetlights, and several of those didn't work, leaving the streets and sidewalks dark and gloomy. An urban wasteland, the only people who frequented the area were the homeless and people who had to pass through on their way to or from somewhere else.

"All right. Check the map for your search sectors and get going. I want you to be as thorough as you can. If you don't find anything, do it again. Look for things you didn't look for the first time."

"I want anyone in the area who appears to not have legitimate business, or is loitering around, contacted and identified. Anyone could be our suspect, so don't let their looks deceive you. The businessman in a suit is just as likely to be our guy as the homeless man sleeping in the park. If they don't have a good reason for being there, or you are suspicious at all, call for a beat car and have them taken to the office for questioning. Any questions?" Vince said, looking around the room.

"Last thing. Everybody be careful. I want you to check in with me every twenty minutes, without fail. Our suspect is a vicious killer, and I believe he will kill anyone who gets in his way or tries to stop him. You find anything, and I mean anything, out of place, or that doesn't seem right, you call me. If you find an open door, call for back-up before you go in. I don't want anyone hurt, and we don't need any heroes. I'll be out and about roaming the area. We'll be using our Tac 2 channel so make sure you set your radios before leaving the room. All right, let's get going."

As the teams filed out of the room heading for the garage to pick up their cars, Vince dialed Liz's cell number. After five rings it went to her voice mail. "Liz, Vince. Where are you? Call me as soon as you get this, it's important." *Damn,* he thought, *Where the hell are you?*

Chapter 27

Consciousness returned slowly. She opened her eyes and looked around, panic momentarily setting in when she did not recognize her surroundings in the dim light from the small lamp on the floor. The panic changed to fear when she realized she was tied, nude, to a chair in a small trailer, her mouth covered with duct tape. Her head throbbed badly from the effects of the drug he had given her, and if she moved it too quickly, waves of pain cascaded through her skull. She tried to scream, but the sound was muffled by the tape. Struggling against her bonds only made them cut deeper into her flesh. She looked around the trailer, listening carefully, but there was nothing to hear. She began to cry into the tape, hanging her head, her tears dripping onto her bare breasts. She shivered uncontrollably with the cold, and cried for the next half hour before dozing off from exhaustion and the lingering effects of the drugs.

She lost track of time, waking, crying off and on for a while, then dozing for a bit, when the sound of the trailer door opening startled her to alertness. She watched the shadowy figure enter the trailer, closing the door behind him. He flipped on the lights, and turned to face her. Her eyes flew open wide when she saw him. Recognizing him, a brief wave of relief washed over her, but then she began to cry in horror when she saw the knife in his hand.

He looked at her sitting tied to the chair, tears streaming down her face, and felt nothing. Walking up to her, he knelt down, cupped her chin in his hand and looked in her eyes for a full minute before speaking.

"You were warned, Ms. Maltby. I didn't want to bring you here, but you me left no choice. This is your fault, not mine. There was a deal. The coverage we wanted, and the exclusives you wanted. But you tried to take control, to decide how things were going to go."

He stood up and placed the knife on the small table next to the chair. As he pulled on a pair of surgical rubber gloves he continued talking.

"You have to learn, Ms. Maltby, who is in control here. You have to be taught a lesson, and I will be your teacher." Picking up the knife, he turned toward her and said, "Now, the lesson begins."

***

Three hours later, he closed the trunk containing her body and wrestled it onto the hand truck. He wheeled the trunk out the side door and along the warehouse, staying in the shadows as much as possible. Opening the gate in the chain link fence, he carefully looked around the corner of the building, and, seeing the street was empty, quickly wheeled the trunk to the van. He slid it inside, then closed and locked the van doors, and walked back along the side of the warehouse, entering through the side door. Once inside, he sat on the floor and leaned against the wall. He leaned his head back and shut his eyes, lost in thought. *I didn't want to do this,* he thought. *The others had it coming, but she didn't. She didn't need to die, we could have worked it out, I know we could. Why did you make me do this?* Tears welled up in his eyes and trickled slowly down his cheeks. He pressed the heels of his hands to his eyes, trying to stop the flow. A low, guttural moan began to rumble up through his chest, gaining volume until it became a cry of anguish. He banged the back of his head against the metal wall, tapping out a slow beat. He sat there for ten minutes, slowly gaining control over his emotions. When he was in control again, he pulled his cell phone from his pocket and dialed a number. "It's done," he said, when his call was answered. "Yes, I will dispose of the body. Don't worry, I'll take care of it. No, she won't be found. We'll meet tomorrow night. Yes, I will. I will, I said, I'll call. All right. Just let me know where and when."

He disconnected the phone, and angrily threw it across the room. "Fucking asshole," he muttered. Raising his arms and face toward the ceiling he screamed at the top of his lungs for the next fifteen seconds.

Five minutes later, he drove slowly away from the warehouse, heading north on the Embarcadero. Two blocks up the street, he saw two of the task force investigators checking the buildings along the waterfront. He drove by, grinning to himself. He turned right, following the signs to the Bay Bridge, and entered the freeway. He turned the radio on and tuned it to the oldies station. An hour later, he dumped her weighted body in the Napa River north of Vallejo.

***

Vince drove slowly south on The Embarcadero, checking on the task force over his radio, making sure they were all right. He had heard from all the teams in the last few minutes, with nothing to report. They assured him they were still hard at it and would contact him immediately if they found anything. He looked at the warehouses along the waterfront and the abandoned buildings across the street as he passed, wondering where the killer could be, where the crime scenes were. Seeing two of the patrol officers he'd had reassigned to him, Mattox and Coleman, he stopped and called them over to the car.

"Nothing so far?" he said, yawning.

"Not yet, Inspector. So far all the buildings in our area seemed secure, but some of them we were unable to get into or see inside. We checked all the doors and windows, but none seemed tampered with or appeared forced."

"You taken a break yet? Anything you want?"

"No break yet, but we sure could use some coffee."

"Okay. I'll be back in about ten minutes. I'll meet you at the corner, by that warehouse on Pier 34."

"Thanks, Boss."

After Vince drove off, the two officers walked to the warehouse and checked the front doors, finding them secured with a rusty chain and lock. They did not appear to have been opened in months. Mattox shook the doors, making sure they were secure. They walked along the front of the building, peering into the filthy windows, unable to see inside. Wiping the window with their sleeves did no good, as the inside was just as dirty and shining their lights on them did no good, either. They tried to see down the darkened side of the warehouse, but their flashlights would not provide enough light to see all the way down.

"Whose turn is it to climb the fence?" Mattox asked.

"It's yours, and you know it," Coleman replied, grinning. "I went over the last one, remember? Ripped my pant leg on the wire."

"Yeah. I was hoping you forgot. Here." Mattox said, handing Coleman his flashlight. "Toss it over when I get on the other side."

Mattox climbed up the chain link, using one of the poles and the side of the building for support. He stepped on the barbed wire across the top and balanced himself, then jumped the eight feet down to the ground on the other side. Coleman tossed the flashlight over and Mattox deftly caught it. Switching it on, he cautiously walked along the side of the building, shining his light in the windows as he passed. A sudden squeal startled him, and he swung his light toward the sound. The light picked up a couple of rats running away from him along the side of the building. *I don't know who is more scared,* he thought, *you or me!* He took a deep breath, then continued walking toward the back of the warehouse. He unsnapped his holster and kept his hand on his pistol, just to be safe. He came to a small door near the end of the warehouse secured with an old, rusted hasp and padlock, and shined the flashlight on the lock. The door was dirty and damp, but Mattox noticed the keyhole in the padlock was shiny, and the knob was cleaner than the rest of the door. He pulled on the padlock, finding it was locked, and shined his light in the small window next to the door. Unable to see inside, he leaned into the door with his shoulder, testing it, finding it was solid, with no play. He walked to the end of the warehouse and checked the back of the building. There were no doors, just a couple of dirty windows he couldn't see through, just like the others. He walked to the end of the pier and shined his light into the water. He didn't expect to see anything, but he wanted to be thorough, in case anyone asked if he checked. He shrugged his shoulders and walked back to the front of the building.

"Anything?" Coleman said, catching the flashlight Mattox threw over the fence.

"Not really. Just one thing struck me odd, though. The door near the back..."

"Wait. Here comes Torelli with our coffee. C'mon, hurry up." Coleman then began walking toward Torelli's car, which had parked at the curb. Mattox shook his head, and climbed over the fence. Before he could get to the car, Coleman had taken the coffee from Vince and started walking back as Torelli drove off.

Chapter 28

Vince read over the task force reports from the night before. So far, each one had been short and reported nothing of consequence. One team working the waterfront near the Ferry Building had interviewed a couple of the homeless men who lived in the area and one had told them of a grey van that had been parked in front of an unused warehouse nearby during the night. He said the van had arrived around 10:30 p.m., and left about 1 a.m. He said he saw a man from the van carry something bulky into the building, which had faint lights on inside. He did not hear anything unusual, and did not get the license plate. Vince put the report aside, planning to assign it to one of the investigators for follow up then continued reading through the other reports, until he got to the report written by Officer Mattox. He read about the padlock and doorknob on the side door and sat up in his chair. It was the only information that seemed promising, and the only location that filled all the categories he was looking for in the murder scene. Rereading it, he smiled to himself and picked up the phone. He thumbed through the city directory until he located the name of the chief redevelopment officer. He dialed the number and leaned back in his chair while it rang. After five rings, the call went to an automated answering system. Vince swore softly at the recording that the office was closed for the day, to leave a message and the call would be returned the next day. He left a message with his office and cell numbers, asking to be called as soon as possible the next morning.

He decided to have the task force go back to watching the killer's possible targets, and at that afternoon's briefing, would re-assign them to their original stakeouts.

A few minutes before the briefing, Vince had received a call from Steve Jacobs. "Bad news, Vince."

"I don't want to hear that, Steve."

"Sorry, pal, but that unidentified print didn't match any that I lifted from the stuff you gave me. Can I safely say I won't be getting anymore requests like this from you?"

"Yeah, you can. Hey, thanks, Steve. I owe you."

"No problem, Vince. See ya."

Vince hung up the phone and leaned back in his chair, thinking. His thoughts were interrupted by the arrival of the task force members.

At the briefing, Vince did not tell them about Mattox's report. He had decided to keep an eye on the warehouse at Pier 34 himself. In case one of the task force members was the leak, or even the killer, he did not want to tip him off. He would stake it out. It was the best lead he had so far, and he felt it was worth following up on.

"Keep close watch tonight. I got a feeling our suspect is going to try to take another victim. My radio will be on, so call me the second anything unusual happens. All right, ladies and gentlemen, let's go to work."

***

He drove slowly along Washburn Street, a half a block behind his quarry. It was dark along the street, and he drove with his headlights off. He pulled to the curb a hundred feet from the bar entrance and watched him go in. He settled back to wait, knowing his target would be inside drinking for the next hour. He looked at his watch and saw it was 9:22 p.m. He would take him as he walked back to his room at the rundown hotel three blocks away. He sat in the van, the engine running and the heater on. It was cold outside. The fog had arrived, and his windows soon became covered with moisture. He wondered why it was necessary to take another victim this soon. *Am I being set-up?* he wondered. He kept looking around, trying to see if there were any police in the area, perhaps sneaking up on him. All was quiet on the street. There were no unusual cars parked along the street, or people wandering about, and after a few minutes, he started to relax. *This should be easy,* he thought. *He isn't on the Task Force list, so no one will be watching him.*

***

Vince parked across the street from the warehouse and Pier 34 at 10:45 p.m. He was shielded by the shadow of the old Hills Brothers Coffee plant and nearly invisible. He sipped from the Styrofoam cup of coffee and looked at his watch. He pulled his cell phone from his pocket and dialed Clark's number.

"Hey, Mike. How's it going?" he asked when Clark answered the call.

"Hi, Vince. Going great. I'm getting along pretty good. Down to one crutch now. I'll be coming back to work starting Monday. Desk duty only, but I'm going crazy here. I'm driving everyone, including myself, nuts."

Vince laughed. "So now you're gonna drive all of us down at the office nuts!"

"Nah, you know what I mean. Anyway, I'll be glad to get back to work. Anything new happening?"

"Actually, yes. I ran everyone's prints again, trying to get a match with that unknown one."

"You did? And let me guess. There was no match, right?"

"Yeah. No match."

"Now will you give up on that?"

"I suppose, but I can't shake the feeling that someone in this office is involved."

"Well, deal with it, Vince, but don't let it interfere with our investigation. Now, what's up?"

"Well, Mattox was checking an abandoned warehouse at Pier 34 and noticed the knob and padlock keyhole on a side door. They were cleaner than the rest of the door, and the lock was shiny, as if a key had been repeatedly inserted."

"Sounds like a good lead. Who you got following it up?"

"Me. In fact, I'm parked across the street right now watching the place."

"What about the rest of the guys?"

"They're back to their babysitting jobs. I told them what I would be doing and where I was, so they can get a hold of me if needed. I got a feeling our killer is going to strike again, and soon."

"You may be right. What about Liz Maltby? Did she turn up yet?"

"Not yet, and I don't have much hope she'll turn up alive."

"Any leads?"

"We're getting phone records from her office and her cell phone in the morning. Maybe that will give us someplace to look."

"Think that will help?"

"Yes, I do. I think she was in contact with the killer, and her phone records may just lead us to him."

"I hope you're right, Vince, but I'm not gonna get my hopes up. This guy is smart."

"Yeah, he is, Mike, but we're smarter. We will get him, and I feel it will be sooner than later. His time is running out."

"Maybe so, Vince. You be careful, Torelli. There's more to this than meets the eye."

"You're right, Mike. I'll talk to you tomorrow."

***

Dennis McClure signaled the bartender to bring another drink. He was slightly drunk already, and figured he could handle one more before going home. He brooded over his glass, talking to no one, thinking of the evening a few months earlier. In need of his daily heroin fix and out of money, Dennis McClure had pulled a ski mask over his face, took a .22 caliber semi-auto from his pocket, and robbed a small store on 6th Street. He took the clerk and his fourteen-year old son to the back room at gunpoint and tied them up. Once he had them on the floor, completely helpless, he shot them twice in the head, killing both. He went back into the store and took the money from the register, all one hundred and twenty two dollars of it, then grabbed a couple of candy bars as he left. He had been questioned by the police and knew he was a suspect in the cime. He also knew it was just a matter of time before he was arrested. He finished his drink, threw some money on the bar, and left. Stopping out in front of the bar, he looked up and down the street. He lit a cigarette, inhaling deeply, then turned and started walking toward his building, his head down.

Right on time, the killer thought. He got out of the van and walked around the back, taking the leather sap from his rear pocket. McClure came shuffling past, looking down, and as he passed, the killer quickly came up behind him and struck him just behind the ear with the sap. McClure dropped like a stone, unconscious. The killer quickly opened the back of the van and lifted McClure inside. Climbing in behind him, he duct taped his hands and feet together. Gagging him with a handkerchief, he secured it with a long strip of tape. He climbed into the driver's seat, and drove off, smiling to himself.

He stopped a few blocks away on a quiet residential street, shutting off the engine. Climbing in the back, he wrestled McClure's body into the trunk, and secured the trunk to the hand truck. Getting back in the driver's seat, he wiped the sweat from his forehead, started the van, and drove to the warehouse. Just as he pulled up in front of the warehouse his cell phone rang. He answered the call as he got out and stood by the driver's door.

"Yes?" he answered. A look of panic crossed his face as he listened to the caller tell him the police were watching the warehouse, and he should not go there.

"But I have my next subject with me now. I'm out front of the building. Okay, I'm outta here," he said, looking up and down the street as he got back in the van and started the engine.

***

Vince saw the van pull up in front of the warehouse, saw the driver get out while talking on a cell phone. He got on the radio and called for backup, then got out of the car and started walking across the street. As he walked, he drew his handgun, holding it down along his leg. The driver suddenly got back in the driver's seat and started the engine. Vince ran across the street, stopping twenty feet in front of the van, aiming his weapon at the driver through the windshield.

"Turn off the engine!" he shouted. "Put your hands out the window where I can see them."

Instead of complying, the driver accelerated quickly toward him, and Vince saw he had his left arm out the window, holding a gun pointed in his direction. He started firing at Vince as he accelerated forward, not aiming, and all but one bullet missed.

Vince felt the bullets snapping by, then a sharp tug to his right side. He fired three quick shots into the windshield, and dove to his right as the van passed. He was barely able to get out of the way, and the van brushed by him, hitting his left leg, causing him to strike his head on the pavement. Vince quickly got to his feet, fighting dizziness, and fired three more shots at the back of the van as it accelerated down the Embarcadero away from him. Blood ran down the side of his face from a laceration on his head, though the dizziness quickly passed. It was difficult to stand on his injured leg and his side burned. He saw the van start to swerve after a half a block, then run up onto the curb and strike a concrete pillar, flipping onto its side and sliding another fifteen feet before stopping. He started limping toward the overturned van, but was only able to take a half a dozen steps before his leg gave out. As he sank to his knees, he could hear sirens approaching. He sat in the middle of the street, placing his hand to his side. He felt a warm dampness, and pulled his hand away. Looking at his fingers, he could see the bright red blood covering them.

After a half a minute, Vince slowly got to his feet, testing his leg. He found that though it was painful, he could walk on it with some effort. He stood in the middle of the street, his face raised to the night sky, listening to the approaching sirens. It had begun to rain softly, and the cool drops felt good on his face. He turned toward the van and began walking slowly toward it, covering it with his pistol. Suddenly the back door burst open and a bloody figure crawled out, carrying a large semi-auto pistol. Seeing Vince, he raised the gun and fired three quick shots, then turned and ran around the van toward the old coffee factory.

Vince dove to the ground when he saw the gun come up, and all the shots passed harmlessly above him. He saw the shooter run around the van toward the buildings, and got to his feet and limped after him. He lost sight of him as the driver ran through a walkway toward the back of the factory and turned the corner. Following the driver, he slowed as he neared the end of the walkway, carefully looking around the corner. Two shots ran out from across the open patio, the bullets striking the bricks near his head, spraying his face with dust and chips. Vince saw the shooter, thirty feet ahead of him, run to the end of Beale Street, then toward an empty lot that led to Brannan. Vince came around the corner, dropped to one knee and carefully aimed at the running figure. He fired three more controlled shots, and saw the suspect stumble, then regain his balance, run onto Brannan Street, turning right, and disappearing around the corner. Vince tried to get up, but his injured leg failed him. He struggled to get to his feet again and limped after the driver. When he got to Brannan, he flattened against the wall of the corner building and cautiously looked around the corner. He didn't see the suspect, but several cars and trash bins along the street could provide cover, making them good ambush sites. He waited a few seconds, listening. Not hearing anything, he chanced a quick turn around the corner, limping as quickly as he could to cover behind a car parked close by. He caught sight of movement out of the corner of his eye, and looked up the street, just glimpsing someone running around the corner onto Stanford Street.

Vince limped up Brannan, but by the time he got to Stanford, the suspect was nowhere to be seen. He remained at the corner, listening and looking, but did not hear or see anything. Looking down, he saw a dark wet splotch on the ground. Looking closer, he saw it was fresh blood. *So, I got you, didn't I, you bastard,* he thought. *I hope it hurts like hell.* He turned and walked painfully down Brannan Street, holstering his weapon, toward the Embarcadero where the back up units had arrived at the scene of the crash, their red and blue lights reflecting off the rain. Vince waved at the officers, holding his badge in the air to identify himself, then collapsed in the street, the shock and pain of his wounds overcoming him. He rolled onto his back, feeling the cool rain on his face. He heard voices approaching as he faded into unconsciousness.

Chapter 29

Vince awoke to the sound of the nurse drawing back the curtain around his bed. He tried to sit up, but the pain in his side made him lie back down.

"Oh, good. You're awake," the nurse said, walking to the window and opening the blinds.

"How long have I been asleep?" Vince asked, yawning. His side ached badly, and there was a dull throbbing in his leg. He had an incredible headache on top of everything else.

"Six hours. The doctor checked you out, found no life threatening injuries, and admitted you for the night for observation. He'll be by in a couple of hours to check on you. Said you could go home this afternoon if everything was still okay."

Vince had a deep bruise to his leg where the van struck him, and one of the bullets had creased his side, causing a painful, but not serious wound. He suffered a slight concussion when his head hit the pavement, and it took seven stitches to close the cut on his scalp.

"Can I get you anything, Inspector?" the nurse asked, as she fitted the blood pressure cuff around his arm.

"Something to drink would be good."

"What would you like?"

"How about a brandy and seven?"

The nursed smiled at him and said, "One orange juice coming right up." She removed the cuff and was rolling it up when Maggie walked into the room.

"Is he behaving?" she asked as she walked over to the bed and kissed Vince on the forehead.

"The perfect patient," the nurse replied.

"Well, I don't believe it. I know him, and he's never perfect. He's up to something and needs watching."

"Actually, he just woke up so he hasn't had time to get into trouble." She smiled at him and winked at Maggie. "I'll get your juice. Don't stay long, Mrs. Torelli. He needs rest. If everything is still okay this afternoon, he can leave here around three."

"I'll just be a minute." She waited until the nurse had left the room, then took Vince's hand in hers. "How you feeling, Babe?"

"I'm sore and tired, but I'll be all right. I need some sleep."

"I know, Hon." Tears formed in her eyes. She took a tissue out of her purse and dabbed at her eyes. "This is getting to be a bad habit, you know, me coming down to the hospital to check on you."

"I know, honey. I'm sorry to put you through this."

"Don't be, Babe. I knew what I was getting into when I married you. It's just hard to see you like this."

"I'm all right, Hon. I'll be out of here today, and home with you and the kids for a few days."

"You better believe it! You're not going anywhere for a while." Wiping her eyes and nose, she said, "I've got to go home for a bit, get the kids off to school, then I'll be back. You rest while I'm gone." She kissed him again on the forehead, kissed his hand, and left the room.

Vince was dozing an hour later when the sound of someone arriving woke him.

"Hey, Torelli," Clark said, as he limped in, leaning on his crutch. He sat in the chair next to Vince's bed. "How ya doin', cowboy?"

"Hey, Mike. Glad to see you're getting around better."

The nurse came in and placed a glass of orange juice on his tray, looked at his chart, then left, closing the door behind her.

"Yeah. I'm healing quickly, so the Doc gave me a walking cast. Glad to be rid of one of the crutches. Thought you'd like to know we found the murder scene."

"Oh, yeah? I'll bet it was that warehouse, pier, what was it, 34?"

"Right again, Batman. Found a small trailer inside. He'd sound proofed it so no one outside could hear what was going on. Lots of dried blood. Forensics took several samples and I'm willing to bet we'll match them with some, or all of our victims."

Clark got up and looked out the door, then closed it again and sat back down. Reaching inside his jacket, he pulled two beer cans out. Handing one to Vince, he popped the top of his and took a long swallow. Vince smiled, shook his head, popped his can open and took a sip. The cold beer tasted good and he savored the first mouthful.

"You must be a mind reader, Mike. Just before you came in, I was dreaming of an ice cold beer, and lo and behold, my dream came true."

"Well, I found there ain't much a cold beer can't fix."

"Get any prints from the crime scene?"

"Yeah. Preliminary match was made about an hour ago. You ain't gonna believe who's prints they are."

"Try me."

"Okay. How about Robert Cullin."

"Robbie? You got to be kidding me!"

"Nope. His prints were all over the place. They also found a bunch of plastic bags in the water off the end of the pier. The dive team retrieved them and inside was coveralls, gloves, shoes, all covered with blood. We found four bags. The lab is testing them now to try and match them with the victims. I'm sure they're gonna find Cullin's DNA on the clothing, too. That will lock it up."

"Four bags? That's odd."

"Why's it odd, Vince?"

"There were five murders. Why isn't there a fifth bag?"

"There were only four, Vince."

"No, Mike. Think about it. Barajas, that kid Ballinger, Sachs, and Gibbs. Then there was Liz Maltby. Also Machado, but we know he wasn't killed there. Should be five bags."

"Oh, yeah. Forgot about her. By the way, we found his almost sixth victim tied up in the back of the van. Got banged up in the crash, but he'll be okay."

"Can he I.D. Cullin?"

"Nope. Said he never saw his assailant. Got hit from behind, and was knocked cold."

"Have we caught him yet?"

"Not yet. Went by his house but he wasn't there. His car is gone, too. That may be what he used to get away last night."

"He's hurt, Mike. I know I hit him at least once, maybe got two into him, plus he got banged up in the crash."

"Yeah. We're checking all the Bay Area hospitals. I've got a guy checking the hospitals up north, too, since he has some family there. An all points bulletin has been sent out to all the neighboring agencies, including the east and south bay. If he's out there driving around, someone will spot him. So far, though, no trace of him."

"We need him alive, Mike. We need to talk to him, find out why he did this."

"Then we need to find him quickly. If he's hurt as bad as you say, we've got no time to lose."

"So why are you here bothering me? Get back to work and make yourself useful," Vince said, grinning at his friend.

"Yessir, drill sergeant," Clark said, standing at attention and saluting. "I'm outta here. Call me if they don't let you out and I'll bring the car around back. We'll make a break for it."

"Will do, partner."

Chapter 30

Vince was released from the hospital by the doctor later that afternoon. Maggie drove him home and got him settled in his chair in front of the television. Making sure he had everything he needed, she told him she had to go pick up the boys after their soccer games and would be back in a couple of hours. Vince took his pain medication, then turned on the ball game. The Giants were playing the Dodgers at Candlestick Park, and were leading three to nothing after two innings. He put the recliner back and settled in. He was still tired and sore, and coupled with the medications, fell asleep a few minutes later.

Vince didn't know how long he slept, but awoke to someone prodding him on the shoulder.

"Wake up, Vince, wake up."

He opened his eyes and saw the barrel of a gun a few inches from his face. Looking up, he saw Cullin standing there, holding the weapon in his left hand. He swallowed hard, finding his voice, and whispered, "Hey, Robbie."

Cullin had placed a chair a few feet away facing Vince. He backed slowly to the chair and sat down heavily. Vince saw he was holding his stomach and his shirt was blood soaked. He had dried blood on his face and neck, his hand was bloody, and he was sweating and breathing heavily.

"You're hurt, Robbie. Let me call for some help," Vince said, starting to get up from his chair.

"Stay there," Cullin yelled, raising his gun and pointing it at Vince's head. "You're not calling anyone, now sit down." The effort seemed to take a lot out of him, and his eyes rolled back in his head momentarily. He quickly regained control and stared at Vince.

"Okay, Robbie. Take it easy, alright?" Vince said, sitting back in his chair. He watched him for a few seconds. "What do you want, Robbie?" Vince spoke softly, as soothingly as he could.

"I don't think I have much time, Vince. I'm trying to hang on as long as I can. There's so much we need to talk about."

"Yes, there is. I've got a million questions for you."

Vince slowly slid his hand down the side of the chair, reaching in the side pocket. He gripped his cell phone, hoping he had left it on. Counting the buttons, he pressed the speed dial for the 9-1-1 setting. He could hear the slight beeping as the phone automatically dialed the number, silently breathing a sigh of relief. He hoped Cullin wouldn't hear the sounds as the phone dialed. He gently dropped the phone the few inches to the floor, hoping it would land face up. It made no noise as it settled on the carpet.

"I'm tired, Vince. So tired. I just want this to be over."

"It can be, Robbie. All you gotta do is give me the gun, and let me call you some help."

"I can't do that, Vince. I can't go to prison. I'm afraid of going to prison."

"I know, Robbie. You know I can't promise you that won't happen, but maybe you could use an insanity defense."

"I'm not crazy, Vince," Cullin said, hanging his head. He had lowered the gun until it was pointed more at the floor than at Vince, but Vince knew his injured leg made rushing Cullin a suicidal act. He could barely walk on it, much less run.

"I'm not saying Robert Cullin is crazy. What I am saying, as an SFPD Homicide Inspector, is that if you surrender as the Retribution Killer, and give a statement how the pressures of your office caused these uncontrollable rages, then maybe there could be a diminished capacity defense. The Retribution Killer may end up spending his time in a mental facility, not a prison."

Vince talked a bit louder than normal, and kept repeating Cullin's name and "Retribution Killer", hoping the dispatcher on the other end of his 911 call would hear him and put it all together. He knew his phone number would automatically be displayed at the 9-1-1 terminal, and the dispatcher would soon have help on the way. Vince also saw that Robbie had placed the chair so that he had his back to the front window, and could not see anyone out front.

Cullin coughed, and a trickle of blood dribbled from the corner of his mouth. He wiped it away with his sleeve. "That's not going to happen. Let's talk, then I'm leaving. But I'm warning you, Vince, as much as I like you, I will kill you if you get in my way. I've already killed four people, and I'll kill again if I have to."

"Robbie. I believe you. Answer a question for me. Why did you do this? You were in a position to put these people away." Vince thought hard to keep their conversation going as long as possible, in case help was on the way. The last thing he wanted was for Robbie to leave before they got there. He felt that Robbie would not shoot him unless he felt threatened, so he kept his voice calm and made no sudden movements.

"That's just it, Vince. Time and again, I had to stand by while cases like these got dismissed on a ridiculous technicality, or weren't filed for some stupid reason. Then, when we had a good case, I never got the chance to prosecute it. I was relegated to a desk, to do grunt work while some ass kissing incompetent was given the assignment. It made me crazy, to where I could hardly stand it. I wanted to make the District Attorney my first victim, but then the opportunity came along to make a difference. I was given the chance to make things right. I took that chance, Vince, and I would do it again."

"But how did it all start, Robbie? I find it hard to believe that you changed that much just from the few years you worked in the D.A.'s office. There must be something more, maybe a family member victimized?"

"How'd you know that, Vince?"

"Just made an educated guess, Robbie. Most times it takes an event like that to set someone on the path you chose."

Cullin hung his head and said nothing for a few moments. When he looked up at Vince, there were tears in his eyes.

"When I was growing up, I idolized my cousin Frank. He was three years older than me, and a great athlete. Played quarterback for our high school, was on the baseball team, always had the best-looking girl friends. He was the coolest guy in school. And you know what, Vince?"

"What, Robbie."

"He always had time for me. Always let me tag along with him and his brother. He defended us to his other friends when they complained because we were with them. He was my hero." Cullin's voice caught in his throat, and a single soft sob came out. "He always looked out for the little guy. That's what got him killed." Cullin sobbed quietly for a bit, then took a deep breath and wiped his eyes on his sleeve. "He got killed trying to help another guy. Stabbed to death. They never got the killer. I swore an oath at his funeral that I would do everything I could to catch his killer, and put him away forever," he said, almost in a whisper. "That was over twenty years ago."

"And they never caught the killer, Robbie?"

"No. But that's why I joined the D.A.'s office, so I could do something about people like the guy that killed Frank."

"But you never got the chance, did you?"

"No, I never did," Cullin said in a half whisper. "I was never given the chance."

Vince glanced out the window while Cullin was talking and saw the police department had sent its

SWAT team. He caught a glimpse of the team members as they took their positions across the street, fading out of sight behind the shrubbery and the cars parked near by until they were almost invisible. He noticed the upstairs bedroom window of the house across the street was open and the curtains had been pulled aside. Though no one was visible in the room, he knew a sniper team was set up there and probably watching him and Robbie through their scopes. He nodded slowly, hoping to let them know he was aware they were there.

Cullin got up from his chair and began pacing back and forth, getting more and more agitated as he talked. Still holding his side with his injured hand, he began waving the gun around with his other one.

"Too many people suffer at the hands of these fucking lowlifes, Vince. Something had to be done, and I was the one chosen to do it. I would have done more, but you were always in my way. How the fuck did you always seem to be in the right place at the right time? Why were you parked next to Clark that night I crashed into you? How did you know I put that kid at the high school? You didn't know I saw you there, did you? I could have, no, I should have, killed you then. It would have been so easy. I like you, Vince, but you were always in the way. You're still in the way. If it wasn't for you, I'd still be doing our work."

"Take is easy, Robbie. I was only doing my job. It was never personal. I never knew it was you, and it was just chance that put me in your way." Trying to distract him, Vince said, "You had me fooled, Robbie. I never suspected you. I felt it had to be someone in our office, but never thought it was you. That was pretty smart of you."

Robbie looked at him and smiled. "It was smart wasn't it. I did fool you, didn't I?"

"Yes, Robbie, you did. Answer something for me. You said you killed four people, but there were more murders than that. Why only admit to four? What about the other two? And what did you mean you were given the chance to do something? Is there someone else involved? Someone pulling the strings?"

Cullin stopped pacing and faced Vince, his back to the front window. "You already know the answer to that, don't you?"

Vince could see fresh blood seeping between Cullin's fingers, and saw him wince in pain. "You're bleeding again, Robbie. Please, let me call for help."

Cullin looked at Vince and raising the pistol, said, "I'm bleeding because of you, Vince. You shot me. Maybe I'll repay the favor. Yeah, maybe I'll just shoot you." Cullin suddenly put the gun to his head and said, "Or maybe I'll just finish what you started."

"Don't do that, Robbie. We can work this out."

"Work it out, Vince?" Cullin made a sound that sounded like a cross between a cough and a laugh. Vince didn't know which it was. "I'm as good as dead, Vince. If I go to prison, I'm a dead man. Maybe I would get the death penalty. Maybe the other prisoners will kill me. Whatever, my chances don't look good. I can't survive in prison."

"You don't know that for sure, Robbie. Nothing is certain in this world."

"The only thing that is certain right now is that a dead man is standing in front of you. Sooner or later, I will be dead." Cullin coughed again, more blood trickling from his mouth. He pressed his hand harder to his side, doubling over. Blood was now dripping from between his fingers, a small pool forming on the floor at Cullin's feet.

Vince started to get up from his chair, causing Cullin to straighten up quickly, pointing his gun at Vince's chest. "Don't move! I will shoot you, Vince."

Vince sat back down. "Robbie, I am going to ask you once more to drop the gun. Let me call some help for you."

"I can't, Vince."

"Look out the window behind you, Robbie. It's over. You can't escape."

Cullin slowly turned around. Looking out the window, he obviously saw the heavily armed SWAT team members out front, half hidden behind the cars, poles and landscaping along the street. He turned back around and looked at Vince, with a half grin on his face. Coughing again, he said, "I guess you're right, Vince. I never thought I would leave this house alive anyway." Tears started rolling down his cheeks. "Goodbye, Vince," Cullin said softly. He slowly raised his pistol and pointed it at Vince.

"No, Robbie!" Vince shouted, struggling to rise from his chair. He knew what Cullin was planning. He tried to get to him, to push him away from the window, but before he could, a single bullet shattered the window and struck Cullin high up on his back, between the shoulder blades. The bullet came out the front of his chest, spraying Vince with blood. Cullin took one step forward, a shocked look on his face, then crumpled to the floor. Vince limped over to him and knelt by his side, feeling Cullin's neck for a pulse. He found it, slight and irregular. He pressed his hand over the wound to Cullin's chest, trying to stem the flow of blood, then pulled him onto his lap, cradling his head on his arm. Cullin opened his eyes, looked at Vince, smiled, and died.

Chapter 31

Five hours later, the crime scene investigators and coroner were done at the house, Cullin's body had been removed, Vince had given a preliminary statement, and he was sitting on the couch next to Maggie. The boys had been picked up by Maggie's mother and taken to her house for a couple of days. Maggie was holding his hand and stroking his arm, her head resting on his shoulder.

"Mike called a few minutes ago, Honey. Asked if it was okay for him to come over tomorrow. I told him it was, but not too early. He and Sandy are coming." Lifting her head, she looked at him and asked, "Are you okay, Babe?"

"Yeah, I'm all right. Just tired."

"You want anything? Want me to fix you something to eat?"

"No, thanks, Hon. I could use a beer, though."

"Okay. Be right back," she said, kissing him on the cheek.

She got up and went into the kitchen. Vince could hear her sobs through the partially closed door, knowing how worried she had been about him.

Vince leaned back on the couch, resting his head against the back. *It doesn't add up,* he thought, *something's missing. He said he did four murders, but there were five, maybe six, including Liz Maltby.* Though her body had not been found, Vince had a gut feeling that she was dead, a victim of the Retribution Killer.

He shook his head, trying to clear the thoughts. It was late and he was very tired. His body ached and he couldn't concentrate on the case. There was still something nagging at him, something he just couldn't quite put his finger on. Vince tried to think about the case, making mental notes of everything he had learned since it broke. Adding what he had found out from Robbie, he was more convinced that Cullin was not the only one involved.

His thoughts were interrupted when Maggie came back in the room. She handed him his beer, then sat next to him. She turned the television on with the remote, and channel surfed until she found an old John Wayne movie, *The Sons of Katie Elder.* They sat there for the next two hours without saying a word.

Chapter 32

They kept coming. No matter how much he fired, they kept coming. Wave after wave, all screaming, running at him, shooting. He could not understand why he had not been shot. He fired and fired until the barrel of his M-16 glowed from the heat of the sustained fire. They got closer and closer. They were almost upon him! He held the trigger down, firing on full automatic. They were upon him, swarming all around, clutching at him...

Vince awoke with his heart pounding, breathing heavily. He sat up with a start and looked around wildly for a moment, until he realized he was alone in his own bed. He lay back down, and, wiping the sweat from his forehead, closed his eyes and willed his body to stop shaking. After a bit, his breathing slowed and his heart stopped pounding. He had just begun to doze off when the telephone rang, startling him. He yelled out, "I got it, Hon," to wherever his wife was. He picked up the receiver, answering, "Torelli." Glancing at the clock, he saw it was eight forty-five in the morning. The call was from the District Attorney's office. He mostly listened for the next couple of minutes, grunting an "Okay" or "Really" every now and then. When he hung up, he sat back and carefully filed the information in his mind.

A half hour later, he received a second call from the Marin County Sheriff's Office Records Supervisor with some information he had asked for. He gave them his office fax number.

He called Lt. Simon, filling him in on what he had found out. "I know Cullin didn't do all the murders. There is someone else involved."

"Are you sure, Vince? It looks to me this case may be closed."

"I'm sure, Boss."

"Any ideas on who the other suspect may be?"

"Maybe. I'm not sure, but I think it may be someone connected to him, probably through his office. I think I may be able to find a link, though. I'm coming in tomorrow morning. There's some stuff in the files I need to find."

"You feeling up to coming in, Vince?"

"That's not a consideration. We need to end this as soon as possible."

"Okay. See you in the morning."

"Thanks, Boss. See you tomorrow."

"Oh, and Vince?"

"Yeah, Boss?"

"If I think for a second that you aren't up to this, I'll send you home, got it?"

"Got it."

***

The next morning, Vince painfully crawled out of bed. He did a few stretching exercises, then limped to the bathroom. After he showered and shaved, he felt better. He still ached, but the pain was manageable and he was able to move around better. He dressed, grabbed his keys and told Maggie, over her protests, he would be back in a couple of hours.

"I've got to go in, Honey. There's no other way."

"I don't like this, Vince. You are in no shape to drive to the City. At least let me drive you."

"No, Hon. You need to stay here, look after the boys."

"I guess you're right, but I don't like it. Please be careful, though. If you get too tired, call me and I'll come and get you."

"I will." Vince kissed her, then hugged her tight for a few seconds. "I love you," he said, before walking out the door.

Vince drove on autopilot, his mind on the case. He reviewed everything he knew about the case up to now, including what he had learned from Robbie. Before he knew it, he was pulling into the parking lot of the Hall of Justice.

The first thing he did when he got to his desk was to make two phone calls. The first was to the District Attorney's office, requesting Robbie's personnel file. They said it would be delivered within the hour. The second call was to the Sonoma County Sheriff's Office. He requested they fax him a copy of an unsolved homicide report in which a victim named Frank was stabbed to death. He was told it would take a couple of hours, and they would call him before faxing the report.

Lt. Simons walked over to his desk carrying two cups of coffee. Sitting on the edge, he handed one to Vince and asked, "How ya doing, Vince?"

"I'm doing all right. Waiting for a couple of reports."

"I still find it hard to believe it was Cullin."

"It makes sense now, Boss. Remember when Mitch Ballinger was taken from the van on the way to Atascadero? Remember the phrase the Deputy said the kidnapper used?"

"No, I don't."

"The kidnapper said, 'Make it so'. That's the same thing he said to Liz Maltby in his calls to her. It's from the TV series, *Star Trek, The Next Generation.* My kids told me that Captain Picard always said it. Robbie was a Star Trek fan, what they call a Trekkie. He told me he has all the episodes of all the programs, and all the movies. Goes to the conventions, too."

"That's right! Now I remember. And I just wrote it off to his being a bit of a geek."

"I should have seen it sooner, Boss. Might have been able to save a couple of the victims."

"Don't blame yourself, Vince. I didn't catch it either. Neither did Mike. Nobody did."

"Liz got several calls from the suspect, Boss. She knew it was the killer calling, and I think she figured out it was Cullin. I don't know how she figured it out, though she could have been bluffing. I think that's why she was killed."

"Yeah, I'd bet you're right. By the way, her blood was found at the crime scene. A lot of her blood. We haven't found the body yet."

"You won't, either. They didn't want her to be found, not like the others," Vince said, sipping from his coffee mug.

"How come we didn't get a hit on the print on Sach's body?" Simons asked.

"Somebody switched Robbie's print card. I think it was Robbie, but he had to have help. I think they got some prints from someone who has no record, doesn't have prints on file anywhere, put Robbie's information on it, then replaced Robbie's real prints with those. They knew Robbie had left his print on the body. The crime lab identified which finger it had come from, so they rolled the same print on one of those sticky tabs and put it over Machado's print. The print guys identified it as Machado's, and nobody questioned it. Look how much time we spent trying to track down Machado when we should have been looking for the real killers."

Simons chuckled. "Pretty smart. They had us following the proverbial wild goose."

"That they did, Boss. And they did it well."

Vince saw a young man in an ill-fitting suit approaching his desk carrying a file folder. "I'm from the D.A.'s office. I have a file for an Inspector Torelli. Can you tell me where to find him?"

Vince smiled at him and said, "You're looking at him. That Cullin's personnel file?"

"I don't know. I'm just a legal aid and was told to bring this to you. I wasn't told what was in it."

"Thanks, kid," Vince said, taking the file from him. He turned to Simons. "You mind, Boss?"

"I know when I'm not wanted. You will keep me informed, right?"

"You bet. Let's hope this gives me what I need to find Cullin's partner. He's the one pulling the strings."

"Think so?" Simons asked.

"Yep. Cullin struck me as being very gullible. He's not a leader, a planner. He could easily be used by the second guy to do the dirty work. He told me at my house, before he died, that the reason he was killing them was his cousin was killed and the killer was never caught."

"So?"

"So, he told me he idolized him, that he was his hero. I think this other suspect had the same effect on Robbie. I also think he had the same ideas about justice as Robbie did. That's why they hit it off, why they hooked up and did what they did. I think this other person knew Robbie idolized him and took advantage of it. He was the one telling Robbie who to kill. He was the planner, the mastermind behind this."

"Well, whoever he is, I have to agree with you that he's someone who knows a lot about the case."

"And something else, Boss. I think this other person is responsible for two of the murders."

"What makes you think that?"

"Robbie told me about the murders he committed. He said he did four of them, not six. I think he did Ballinger, Sachs, Gibbs, and Liz Maltby. I think this other guy did Barajas and Machado."

"That so? What makes you think that?"

"Well, Machado's body was found floating in the bay, shot in the head, and we haven't found Liz's body. With all the others, they wanted the bodies to be found. They put them where they would be found easily. In fact, they put them in places that were very ironic. Ballinger was left at the school where he committed his murders. Sachs' body was left on a bus bench at the intersection where he ran into and killed the family, and Gibbs body was left on the steps of the church where he molested the boys."

"What about Barajas?"

"That puzzles me. He was left in the alley nowhere near where he did the drive-by. I can't figure that out. Why there and not where he shot the kid?"

"Maybe, since it was the first murder, the killer hadn't developed his fine sense of irony. Maybe he got the idea to leave the bodies at the original crime scenes later."

"That's possible, Boss. But it still doesn't seem right to me."

Simons chuckled. "Another of those famous Torelli hunches?"

Vince smiled. "I've learned to trust those hunches."

"Well, keep at it. You get the answers to your questions, you let me know."

"Will do, Boss."

Chapter 33

Vince opened Cullin's file and began reading. What he read only made him more sure that Robbie was not the mastermind behind the killings. What he did find was that Cullin was an unremarkable attorney. He had handled several minor prosecutions for the District Attorney's Office, and, according to his proficiency reports, had done a mediocre job. His supervisors described him as somewhat timid and non-confrontational in court. He was described as "un-remarkable".

His personal information listed his family as living north of San Francisco. Some family members lived in Petaluma, some in Red Bluff and Ukiah. He grew up in a small farming and ranch community between Ukiah and Willits, living on the small farm his grandfather started and his father inherited. He attended Willits High School, graduating 76th out of his class of 123. He was not the athletic sort, and didn't play any sport for his school. He was the type that ran water out to the players during the football game, or perhaps worked the sidelines as a scorekeeper or linesman. His parents were both deceased, his father dying of heart failure eight years ago, his mother five years earlier, a victim of breast cancer.

Robbie had gotten his law degree from the University of the Pacific, McGeorge School of Law, in Sacramento. He finished in the lower third of his class, and went to work for a small law firm in Red

Bluff handling mostly estate planning. After a year and a half, he applied to the District Attorney Offices in Sacramento, Alameda, San Francisco, Contra Costa, Tehama County, Solano, and Mendocino Counties. San Francisco County was the only one to show any interest, and four months later, Robbie was hired as an Assistant District Attorney. He soon earned a reputation for not being the sharpest tool in the shed, and was given mostly busy work assignments. Infrequently, he would be handed a minor criminal case to handle, doing so without distinction. His non-work hobbies included collecting Star Trek memorabilia and old time rock and roll records, going to Star Trek conventions all over the United States, and reading.

Vince wrote down the addresses and phone numbers for Cullin's relatives, in case he needed to contact them. He placed the note in his case folder. The one thing that puzzled Vince was why Cullin had been assigned to his task force. There were undoubtedly many more qualified ADA's, so what made Cullin the one to get the assignment? Vince made a mental note to check into it later.

Vince closed the file and placed it on his desk. He rested his hand on it, as if to keep it from floating away, and leaned back in his chair, deep in thought. His reverie was broken by the sound of his phone ringing. Vince picked up the receiver. "Inspector Torelli," he answered.

"Inspector Torelli, this is Detective Albers with the Mendocino County Sheriffs Office. I've got that report you asked for."

"Oh, good. Can you fax it to me?"

"I don't think so. There's over a hundred and twenty pages. How about if we overnight it to you?"

"Guess that will have to do." Vince looked at his watch, seeing it was 3:45 in the afternoon. "Any chance you can get it out tonight?"

"Doubt it. Even if I did, it wouldn't go until tomorrow morning, so you may not get it until tomorrow afternoon, or even the next morning."

"Tell you what. Hang on to it. I'll drive up there and get it myself."

"You're coming up here?"

"Yep. It's only a bit more than two hours, and I need that report."

"I'll be gone by the time you get here, but I'll leave it in 'will call' for you. You know how to get here?"

"Yeah, I think so. Main office is in Ukiah, right?"

"Yep. Good luck, Inspector. Hope you find what you're looking for."

"Thanks, Detective. I owe you one."

Vince hung up the phone, got up and walked to Lieutenant Simons' office. He knocked on the doorframe and leaned in the open door. "Got a minute, Boss?"

Lt. Simon's looked up from the stack of files on his desk and motioned Vince in. "What's up, Torelli?"

"I need to take a road trip. Mendocino County has my report on that unsolved homicide involving Cullin's cousin, but it's too big to fax. They said they could overnight it, but I need it before then."

"So let me guess. You wanna take a ride up there and get it yourself, right?"

"Gosh, Boss, you are so smart! No wonder you're in charge here!"

"All right Torelli. The ass kissing isn't necessary. Get a car from the motor pool and get going."

"Thanks, Boss. I'll let you know what I find out. I've got a feeling the report is a key ingredient to this case."

"Still looking for that elusive second suspect, eh?"

"Yes, I am. And I will get him."

"I believe you will, Vince." Simons yelled out the door. "Clark, get your gimpy ass in here!" Turning back to Vince he said, "I'm gonna let you do this, but I want you to take Clark with you. Both you guys are too beat up to go alone, but between the two of you, I've got a whole person."

Clark limped into the office. "You bellowed, Lt.?"

"Yes, I did. You're taking a ride with Vince to Mendocino County. He's going up there to get a report. I want you to keep him company."

"All right. You mind if I ask why we are going up there?"

"Vince needs the report on the murder of Cullin's cousin and is too impatient to wait for it to get here, so he wants to drive up there and get it."

"Okay." Turning to Vince he said, "Let me call Sandy and let her know. I'll meet you downstairs."

Vince nodded, then said to Lt. Simons, "I've gotta call Maggie and tell her, then I'm outta here. Talk to you later, Boss."

Vince left the office and went back to his desk. He called Maggie and told her where he was going. "I probably won't be home until around midnight. Mike's going with me, and we'll probably stop for some dinner on the way." Vince listened ruefully while Maggie let him know in no uncertain terms how unhappy she was with him.

"It's just a drive up and back. I promise I'll take it easy," he said, then quickly hung up before she could start in on him again. He wondered again what he had ever done to deserve her.

Chapter 34

Vince and Clark drove north on Highway 101 across the Golden Gate Bridge. The early commuter traffic heading home to San Rafael, Mill Valley, Larkspur and San Anselmo slowed them to no more than twenty-five miles per hour for the first three quarters of an hour of the trip. Traffic began to thin once they passed San Rafael, several miles north of the bridge.

Vince set the cruise control on the white Ford Taurus at 72 miles per hour, then moved the seat back a bit to stretch out his legs, especially his left leg, injured when he was struck by Cullin's van.

Clark was strangely quiet during the ride, looking out the side window, or adjusting the radio volume. Vince stole a couple of glances at his partner and friend while he filled him in on his thoughts of the case, but didn't ask him why he was so quiet. He figured Clark was thinking about the case, absorbing what Vince was telling him and would talk when he was ready. They continued north for the next hour, passing Petaluma, then Santa Rosa.

The drive was scenic, and the late evening light cast shadows along the countryside. The wind picked up and Vince could see the trees along the highway swaying to the rhythm of the gusts. Dark clouds rolled in from the coast, promising a rain shower later that evening. They stopped for dinner at a roadside café in Healdsburg, a little more than half way to Ukiah. Clark was still not talking, other than to order his food, which he hardly touched. He kept staring out the window of the diner, watching the headlights flash by on the highway. When they were done, they walked silently to the car and continued their journey.

After another twenty minutes of driving, Vince turned to Clark and asked, "Everything all right, Mike?"

Without turning, Clark answered, "Yeah, Vince."

Vince looked at his friend. "Something's wrong. You've never been this quiet before. Anything you want to talk about?"

Clark turned around and looked at Vince, a look of misery on his face. "Pull off the highway at the next exit, Vince."

"Pull off the highway? Why? What's up, Mike?"

"Just do it, Vince," Clark said, bringing up his Beretta nine-millimeter pistol and pointing it at Vince's chest.

"Mike! What the hell is going on?"

"Take the off ramp, Vince," Clark said.

"Are you in some kind of trouble, Mike? Is there something I can do to help?"

"Just pull off, Vince."

When Vince slowed and entered the off ramp, Clark said, "That's it. Now, turn right." He guided them to a dirt road that split a large grove of eucalyptus trees and had Vince turn into the grove. Half way through, he told Vince to stop.

Vince pulled off the road and put the car in park, leaving the engine running. "What's going on, Mike?"

"All in good time, Vince. First, hand me your pistol, butt first. Do it slowly and carefully."

"Sure, Mike." Vince slowly reached inside his coat and removed the Smith and Wesson semi auto from his shoulder holster and, with two fingers, handed it to Clark.

"There, Mike. Now, tell me what this is all about."

"You just had to keep pushing, Vince, didn't you? I had it all neatly wrapped up. Everything pointed to Robbie, but you just couldn't accept it. You should have let it go."

"Oh, God, Mike. Don't tell me you're involved in the murders?"

"You would have found out soon enough. You were right about the report being the key to this investigation."

"Why, Mike? What's in the report that would break the case?"

"Remember what Robbie said about his cousin Frank being killed? How he and Frank's brother always tagged along with him?"

"Yeah. He said he was murdered trying to help someone else. The killer was never caught."

"That's right. What the report will tell you is that Robbie's cousin was my brother."

"You're kidding!"

"No, I'm not, Vince. I told you when we first met that my brother had been killed trying to break up a bar fight. Frank was my brother, Vince. Frank Clark."

"So that would mean Robbie was your cousin?"

"Yes. Well, second cousin. His mother was my mother's first cousin. We used to hang out a lot when we were kids, since we were about the same age."

Vince was stunned by this news. The realization that his partner, a cop he had worked so closely with over the last few years, could be involved in the brutal murders was a shock to his mind. All he could think to ask at the moment was, "Why, Mike?"

"I think of my brother every day, Vince. I just can't get over his death. He was my hero, too. He was everything a big brother should be. He loved me and I loved him. He was always looking out for me. And, of course, Robbie, too. He took us with him wherever he went, defended us, made sure we were okay, and always was kind to us, even when Robbie or I pestered him. Especially Robbie." Clark's eyes filled with tears and he wiped his eyes with his sleeve, sniffing. He looked at Vince and said, "I'm sorry you found out, Vince."

"That's my job, Mike. You know that. Its what I get paid to do."

"I thought I had everything covered. Robbie was so willing to help, he'd do anything I asked. He did, in fact."

"Will you tell me about it, Mike? I think you owe me that much." Vince had little doubt as to his fate, once Clark was done talking. His plan now was to keep him talking as long as possible. He needed time to figure out how he would get out of this.

The sky had darkened and clouds coming in from the ocean covered the moon. The surrounding trees prevented any light from the adjacent highway from reaching them. It began to rain, coating the trees and car, cutting what little visibility there was even more. Vince glanced around the car, wondering if he could use the darkness to his advantage, looking for anything he could use as a weapon.

"I got Robbie hired with the DA's office. Called in a couple of favors, applied a bit of pressure. Once he was hired, we kept our family connection a secret. We had been talking a long time about doing this, even before he became an attorney. Planned it all out. When he finished law school and first got hired, they sent Robbie to get fingerprinted. He never went. He had the blank print cards, so he brought a friend of his who had never been arrested or fingerprinted and I rolled his prints on the cards. Robbie filled them out with his information and submitted them as his. That way, if we ever did start up our plan, he wouldn't be identified by prints. I wasn't worried about my prints being found. I knew I wouldn't leave any. When he got hired by our DA's office, he brought the prints with him, and gave them to the personnel office. They accepted them as his and didn't have him re-printed, so he was safe from any possible print identification. Even the FBI print data base had the fake prints."

"Your idea, or his, Mike?"

"My idea, Vince. Robbie isn't capable of planning ahead like that. All he can do is follow orders, and he was good at it."

"So how did you decide to set this up?"

"Robbie identified the first victim, Barajas. We found the abandoned warehouse on the waterfront, and I cut the lock off the back door, replacing it with an old one of my own. There was an old trailer inside that the previous owners must have left behind. We fixed it up, soundproofed it, bolted the chair to the floor. It was the perfect place. No one could see in, and nothing could be heard from outside the building. The perfect place."

Vince cautiously looked around as Clark talked. He saw the faint red glow from the flashlight charger mounted on the floor between the front seats. He could just see the outline of the heavy Streamlight in the charger. He slowly shifted in his seat, sliding toward the center and closer to the flashlight. He let his hand rest on the seat next to him, a scant four inches from the charger. To cover changing his position on the seat, Vince said, "That explains a few things. I never thought Robbie was smart enough to pull this off."

"He wasn't. Like I said, he was good at following directions. I told him what to do. Hell, I even showed him."

"Showed him? How, Mike?"

"When we took Barajas, which was easy, by the way, we took him to the warehouse and I showed him what to do, how to make the cuts. I showed him where to put the number on their cheeks, and showed him how to make the last thrust to the heart."

"How did you get Barajas to the warehouse?"

"I stole a van from Oakland Airport. Had Robbie drive it and follow me to where Barajas was walking home. I was in an unmarked car. All I had to do was show him my badge and tell him to get in the car. When he did, I slugged him with a sap, and Robbie and I transferred him to the van."

"But Robbie made a mistake, didn't he? That was why we got his print off Barajas body."

"Yeah. Dumb shit took off his latex gloves before he dumped the body. Good thing we switched his prints," Clark said, shaking his head side to side. "By the way, you remember when Robbie first showed up at our office?"

"Yeah. What about it?"

"Remember he said he had never been there before, had never worked with any of the inspectors, had never met any of us?"

"Yeah. He didn't know who I was at first. I introduced him to you."

Clark chuckled, saying, "I thought we were had right then. When you introduced us, you introduced me as Inspector Clark. You remember what Robbie said?"

"Oh, shit. He called you by your first name! I should have caught that. How did he know your first name if he had never been there before or met any of us?"

"Yep. I was surprised you missed that."

"I had a lot on my mind at the time. Wasn't really paying too much attention to him."

While they were talking, Vince carefully moved his hand to the flashlight and slowly began sliding it out of the charger, careful to move it only when they were talking to cover any slight noise he might make. He had it almost halfway out before he brought his hand up to the seat so Clark would not notice what he was doing. It was now almost totally dark in the car. The red charger light had gone out as soon as Vince had pulled the flashlight out a couple of inches and the contacts were no longer connected. Vince didn't think Clark would notice what he was trying to do. Changing the subject, he asked, "So, you killed Barajas?"

"Yeah. Robbie did the others. He handled it a lot better than I thought he would. Actually, he got pretty good at it. He even was able to take them himself after Barajas. I guess I under estimated him."

"What about Liz, Mike? You know what happened to her?"

"Yeah. She figured out it was Robbie calling her. Dumb ass! He had to tell someone, had to brag. I don't know how she knew, but she did. She became a liability, one we couldn't afford. Robbie took care of her."

"We never found her body. You know where she is?"

"Yeah. I had Robbie dump her in the Napa River outside Vallejo, off Highway 37, where the bridge crosses the river near Mare Island."

"What about Machado? Did you set him up, too?"

"Robbie thought that one up. I just picked the right person."

"How did you get him to go along with it?"

"A buddy of mine is an instructor at the academy. He was telling me about this recruit they were having problems with. The more he told me about him, the more I was certain he was perfect for our needs. That recruit was Machado. I called him and had him meet us. We told him what we were planning to do and that we knew he felt the same. We asked him to help us."

"In reality, all you did was set him up."

"Yeah. He was easy to convince."

"Why was he killed?"

"Because you got lucky and found where we had stashed him. He had nowhere to hide after he ran from the apartment, so he had to be disposed of to prevent him from turning himself in."

"So you killed him and dumped his body in the Bay?"

"Yeah. The business card was Robbie's idea. I didn't even know he had put it in Machado's pocket until he told me on the way back to the City." Clark chuckled, shaking his head. "Oh, Robbie. Just couldn't stand not bragging about what you were doing, could you."

Vince slid the flashlight out a couple of more inches, realizing it was free of the holder. He gripped the shaft and slowly brought it up. When Clark was not looking, he put it on the seat between his legs, still maintaining his grip on it.

Clark continued talking. "Robbie picked him up after you chased him from the apartment and took him to his place. I went there after work and told him I had a new place for him to stay, somewhere he would be safe, where no one would find him. He went with me, the dumb ass, and I took him to Fort Baker and shot him on the beach. I dumped his body in the bay, and the tide must have carried him to Sausalito."

"So Robbie was telling me the truth. You know, Mike, he never gave you up. Poor kid, still faithful, even though he knew you had given up on him."

Clark laughed softly. "Still faithful, like a little puppy. That's the way he was with my brother. You know, Frank never minded Robbie tagging along with us. At least, he never said he did. But you know what? I hated always having him there. I hated his fawning over Frank, his hero worship. Frank was *my* brother, not his. He had no right to tag along all the time. I got sick of it."

"So why did you two stay so close?"

"After my brother was killed, Robbie was as upset as me, maybe more. We had lost touch for a while after high school. After the funeral, we kind of consoled each other, and as time went on and there was no progress in finding the killer, we got angrier and angrier. After the years went by and they still hadn't identified the suspect, we made a pact to do something about it. Since we couldn't help find my brother's killer, we hit upon a plan to make the scum that somehow escaped the justice system pay for their crimes."

"Playing judge, jury, and executioner, Mike?"

"If that's how you want to think of it, Vince. We looked at it a bit different. We were providing a service to the public, keeping them safe by eliminating the worst criminals. And our citizens didn't even know it."

Vince gripped the flashlight a bit tighter. "What now, Mike? Where do we go from here?"

Clark stared at Vince through the darkness, not answering for a short while. "I don't know, Vince. I need to leave the country, go someplace where there is no extradition. The big question is, what am I going to do about you?"

"I think the bigger question is what about Sandy and Allie? And your baby on the way?"

"It will be better for them if I just disappear. They couldn't take the strain of a long, drawn-out trial, and I can't go to prison. I'd die in there, if I didn't get the death penalty. How long do you think a cop would last in prison, Vince? Not very long."

"You would be in isolation, Mike. They wouldn't put you out with the general population. You would be safe."

"Safe, Vince? Hah! You know they would find a way to get to me. No one is safe in prison."

"Even so, Mike, there's a good chance you won't get the death penalty. If you kill a cop, you will be executed for sure."

"Not if they don't catch me. I can drive back to San Francisco Airport and fly away, to someplace where there is no extradition. I've got my passport with me, and I've been putting money aside just in case. I've got enough to keep me going for a while, and I'll find something to do to earn a living. I've thought about this for quite a while, Vince, and there's only one sure way for me to disappear, and that's to kill you. I like you, Vince. You're the best investigator I've ever seen, and a good friend. I know I wouldn't want you coming after me. No, Vince, there's only one thing to do."

Clark, still looking at Vince, raised the pistol and said, "I'm sorry I have to do this, Vince. I'll make it quick and painless." He extended the gun toward Vince's forehead. "Bye, Vince." He pulled the trigger.

Chapter 35

Vince flung himself back in the seat just as Clark fired the pistol. He could feel the heat of the bullet as it passed in front of is face, shattering the driver's door window. The burnt powder tattooed his cheek, burning him briefly, leaving black stippling on his skin. The hot gases momentarily blinded him, making his eyes tear up and causing him to involuntarily close his eyes tightly.

At the same time he had flung himself back in the seat, he swung the flashlight up from his lap in a back-handed sweep, not seeing where it was going, but hoping to hit something, anything. As luck would have it, the heavy Streamlight struck the pistol in Clark's hand, knocking it toward the back of the car. Clark almost lost his grip on the big semi-automatic from the force of the blow, barely hanging onto the gun. Vince blindly swept the flashlight back toward the front of the car, feeling a solid thunk as it hit Clark on the cheek, stunning him, opening a gash that began to bleed freely, and causing him to drop the gun. Vince scrubbed his eyes with the back of his free hand, trying to rub the tears and irritation away. He could not see Clark very well, but heard him moaning. He groped along the seat, trying to locate his weapon. Unable to find it, he sat up and tried to open the driver's door. Clark was leaning forward, moaning, when he shook his head, suddenly sat upright and let out a blood-curdling scream. He lunged at Vince, grabbing at his face, neck and clothing, anything that was within reach. He got a grip on Vince's coat and was trying to drag him toward him with one hand while punching at him with his other. Vince jammed the gear selector in drive and floored the accelerator. He could see better, though full vision had not yet returned, and his eyes still stung from the burnt gunpowder.

Unlike Clark, Vince had not undone his seatbelt when they first parked in the grove. The car picked up speed gradually, the tires spinning on the wet grass and muddy road. He had no idea where he was going, but he knew he had to do something, and at the moment, he felt it was best to try to get back out into the open. Vince's seatbelt kept Clark from pulling him from behind the steering wheel, and though several of Clark's blows landed, there was not enough room in the car for him to generate much force. Though they stung, even cut his lip, none were strong enough to incapacitate him. Clark continued yanking at Vince, growling noises coming from his throat.

Clark's pulling on Vince's jacket and Vince trying to duck the punches was making him yank the steering wheel back and forth, causing the car to skid across the wet and muddy road. Vince kept the accelerator floored, and by the time they were almost out of the trees, the car was traveling at over 40 miles per hour. Vince aimed the car as best he could toward a large tree near the edge of the grove and kept the car at full throttle. He kept one hand on the steering wheel and fought to loosen Clark's grip on his coat with the other.

Just before the car struck the tree, Vince tried to brace himself for the impact. The collision crumpled the front end of the car, forcing the engine back toward the passenger compartment. The car rebounded almost ten feet from the force of the collision. The air bag deploying and the seatbelt kept Vince in the car and prevented him from being severely injured, but Clark was not so lucky.

The collision with the tree launched Clark toward the front of the car. His legs struck the dashboard, re-breaking his partially healed leg as his head hit the windshield, shattering the safety glass and fracturing his skull. He was ejected through the broken windshield and slammed into the tree head first, breaking his neck. He fell to the base of the tree, dead before he hit the ground.

Chapter 36

Steam arose lazily into the air from the engine compartment of the damaged car, and the only sounds Vince heard were from the rain pelting down, a slight hiss from the radiator, and a slow ticking from the overheated engine.

Vince lay slumped over toward the passenger seat, supported by the seat belt, slightly dazed. He listened to the rain on the roof of the car, and smelled the overheated engine. His body ached from the collision, especially where the seatbelt and shoulder harness crossed his body, and his just healed shoulder and half healed leg flared with new pain. He shook his head to clear his senses, and when full realization of where he was and what had happened returned, he began groping in the darkness in a panic along the seat and the floor for a weapon, realizing Clark was no longer in the car but not knowing where he was. He grew more frantic as he searched, expecting to feel a bullet slam into him at any moment. His hand touched something cold and hard. He gripped it desperately, recognizing the familiar feel of his Smith and Wesson. Sitting up, he looked around wildly. He slid the safety off with his thumb, trusting there was still a bullet in the chamber, as he normally kept the gun.

He could not see out of the shattered windshield. He released his seat belt and tried to open the driver's door, but the crash had wedged it shut. He slid across the seat to the passenger door but found it jammed closed by the crumpled fender. He lay back in the seat and with his good leg, began kicking at the passenger window. After three solid kicks, the glass shattered, spraying the ground with bits of the safety glass.

Vince sat up and looked around quickly, his weapon at the ready, trying to locate Clark, looking for possible hiding places or cover should he need it. He squirmed through the window and fell to the wet, muddy ground, his shoulder and leg flaring with pain at the sudden effort. As quickly as he could, he scrambled to his feet and looked around in the dim light, tracking his gaze with the pistol, which he now gripped two-handed. He could see nothing moving other than the branches of the trees swaying in the wind. He squatted down, using the car for cover and listened for movement, pelted by the heavy raindrops soaking his clothing. He moved slowly and cautiously toward the back of the car, the rain effectively masking any other noise. Checking behind the car, he continued to the driver's side and moved toward the front of the car. As he got near the front of the car, he looked toward the tree, seeing the scar where the car had crushed and splintered the bark, and saw an odd shadow on the ground at the base of the tree. He slowly walked toward it, covering the shadow with his pistol as he approached. After several steps, the shadow morphed into the body of his partner and friend, who had just tried to kill him. From the odd position of his head, it was obvious Clark was dead.

Vince holstered the Smith and Wesson and walked to Clark's body. He knelt down next to him and rolled his friend onto his back, then slid to the ground beside him, sitting on the muddy roadway. He pulled his cell phone from his pocket and dialed 9-1-1.

EPILOGUE
Seven months later

Vince sat in the judge's chambers, listening in disbelief as the judge declared a mistrial due to prosecutorial misconduct. He had been subpoenaed to appear at the trial of a homicide he had investigated two years earlier in which a man had murdered his girlfriend and her two children, ages four and one and a half. Vince had just spent the last two days on the stand testifying.

The trial had been going well, and Vince felt the Assistant District Attorney had presented a solid case. He had tied what little evidence they had to the suspect, and his questioning of the only witness, a 19 year old former girlfriend of the suspect, seemed to provide the final bit of information to ensure a conviction. The girlfriend had testified that one night, after the defendant had consumed half a bottle of Jack Daniels whiskey, he started talking about a former girlfriend, and that he had killed her in a fit of rage. He had started crying, saying how bad he felt about taking her life. He didn't mention her two children he had also murdered. After a short crying jag, and a few more shots of whiskey, he turned to her and told her he would kill her, too, if she ever told anyone what he had said. Since he had already beaten her a couple of times, she figured it would only be a matter of time before she met the same fate.

The next day, as soon as he left for work at a local car wash, she called the police and told them what he had said. Once he was in custody, it was easy to connect him to the murders with the evidence. The police were already looking for him for further questioning, and though they had not specifically named him as a suspect, listed him as a "person of interest".

When Vince arrived back after the lunch break, before the trial continued, the judge had already had the jury removed. He then told the defense attorneys and the ADA handling the case, as well as Vince, to meet him in his chambers. Once they were all gathered, he told them he had received information from the defense team that was of grave importance. It seems the ADA prosecuting the case was having an affair with the suspect's girlfriend and witness to the murders, a fact he failed to disclose to the court or the defense team. The witness had told the sister of the defendant about the affair and the sister immediately informed her brother's defense team, who in turn advised the judge.

In chambers, the judge let his anger loose on the ADA, directing the full force of his outrage against him. He said he would begin disbarment proceedings against the ADA, and would make sure he never practiced law again. The defense team joined with the judge and threatened to go to the press with the story. The judge then turned his wrath on the District Attorney himself, who had been summoned by the judge and had arrived a few minutes earlier.

The judge questioned the future value of the witness' statements, should the District Attorney decide to re-file the case and, since the defense had attacked the validity of the other evidence, once this information became public, the validity of the prosecution's entire case became questionable and the chance of a conviction for murder was extremely doubtful.

Listening to the ADA trying to cut a deal in which the defendant would plead guilty to voluntary manslaughter, and with credit for time served, would spend another two and a half years in prison before becoming a free man, infuriated Vince.

The District Attorney immediately stepped in and told the judge there would be no deal at this time. He said they would have to discuss the issue to see if it was proper and reasonable to re-file the charges, then decide to offer the defendant a deal. He also assured the judge that the ADA was no longer a member of his staff. He agreed with the judge that a mistrial was in order.

Another vicious murder had escaped justice. Vince left the courthouse trembling with anger, his mind in turmoil. As he walked to his car, he shivered involuntarily, a strong feeling of déjà vu coursing through him.

About the Author

John Schembra was born Jan. 3, 1948 and raised in the San Francisco Bay Area.

He retired Feb. 2001 from a small northern California police department as a Sergeant after almost 30 years' service.

Prior to becoming a police officer, he was a Military Policeman assigned for a year to the 557th MP Co., Long Binh, Bien Hoa, South Vietnam, where he had several "adventures" that provided the basis for his first novel, *MP*.

He has earned a B.A in Administration of Justice and an M.A in Public Administration. He spent his retirement time writing as well as teaching other police officers emergency vehicle operation/pursuit driving through the Contra Costa County Sheriff's Office and Police Academy. He also instructs officers in the driving simulators, is a train the trainer for emergency vehicle/pursuit/ simulator instructors, and has been recognized as a Subject Matter Expert by the State of California in emergency vehicle operations/pursuit driving.

He has had several trade articles published in law enforcement magazines such as *Law and Order*, *Police Officer's Quarterly*, and *The Backup*. He is also a member of the Police Writers Association, a very supportive writers' group for anyone affiliated with any type of law enforcement organization.

In his spare time (what little there is) John enjoys reading, fishing, and most of all, spending time with his family.

John's personal website is:
http://www.jschembra.com

You can keep track of John's work on his author website:
http://www.writers-exchange.com/John-Schembra.html

If you want to read more about other books by this author, they are listed on the following pages...

A Vince Torelli Novel

Book 1: MP - A Novel of Vietnam
{War: Vietnam}

June 1967 As Vincent Torelli stepped off the plane at Bien Hoa Air Base, South Vietnam, he was almost overwhelmed by the stench in the hot, humid air. He still had a hard time realizing he was in Vietnam. Drafted into the armed forces five months earlier, he ended up becoming a Military Policeman, assigned to the 557th MP Co. at Long Binh Post just outside Binh Hoa City.

His year tour of duty in Vietnam changes him from a somewhat naive young man to a battle hardened veteran. Through unlucky chance, Vince becomes involved in the ferocious '68 Tet offensive, barely surviving the night. He sees and experiences things he could never have imagined before Vietnam.

This is Vince's story, of how he survived that year in Vietnam, how he coped with the hell he faced, of the friendships he formed, and of the sorrow of lives lost.

Publisher Book Page:
http://www.writers-exchange.com/MP-A-Novel-of-Vietnam.html

Amazon: http://mybook.to/MP
AmazonSmile (US Region):
https://smile.amazon.com/dp/B00440DR4I

Book 2: Retribution
{Mystery: Serial Killer}

There's a vigilante killer loose in San Francisco, and when the justice system fails, he doles out his own brand of justice.

Homicide Inspector Vince Torelli has handled some of the city's worst murders, but this case has him baffled. It seems no matter what he does, the killer manages to stay one step ahead of him, anticipating his every move. Hell, the false clues and trail the killer leaves keeps Vince chasing shadows as the body count rises.

Will he discover the killer's identity? And will he survive long enough to bring him to justice?
Publisher Book Page:
http://www.writers-exchange.com/Retribution.html
Amazon: http://mybook.to/VinceTorelli2
AmazonSmile (US Region):
https://smile.amazon.com/dp/B003YUCBRI

Book 3: Diplomatic Immunity
{Mystery: Serial Killer}

There are sixty-six Consulates and Embassies in San Francisco, and a very talented, deadly sniper is targeting the Consul Generals, seemingly at random.

Homicide inspector Vince Torelli has a reputation for solving the toughest cases in the City, but this one is unlike anything else he has faced. The killings make no sense, lack motive, and appear to be unre-

lated but Vince knows there has to be a link between them. He struggles to find the connection and identify the suspect, but as he gets closer to the answer, he becomes a target himself. This can end only one of two ways, either by him solving the case, or by becoming a victim himself.
Publisher Book Page:
http://www.writers-exchange.com/Diplomatic-Immunity.html
Amazon: http://mybook.to/VinceTorelli3
AmazonSmile (US Region):
https://smile.amazon.com/dp/B007N5BCZM

Sin Eater

{Supernatural Murder Mystery}

The shocking murder of a professor at San Donorio State College brings the city police to investigate, with Campus Police Officer Sarah Ferris as the college liaison.

Sarah's friend, Nico Guardino, a history professor at the college, gets drawn into helping and while Nico and Sarah struggle to find the murderer, the killing continues.

As Nico is inexorably drawn deeper and deeper into the investigation, he begins getting flashes of visions and deep feelings of dread that he knows are somehow connected to the murderer. He feels the connection becoming stronger, but how and why remains unknown. His visions and feelings are becoming more and more disturbing as the investigation progresses...

Publisher Book Page:
http://www.writers-exchange.com/Sin-Eater.html
Amazon: http://mybook.to/SinEater
AmazonSmile (US Region):
https://smile.amazon.com/dp/B01M0TWRHH

Made in the USA
San Bernardino, CA
22 December 2016